Single
GIRL RULES
#BANANA PARTY

BRIDE TO BE

USA TODAY BESTSELLING AUTHOR
IVY SMOAK

This book is a work of fiction. Names, characters, places, and incidents are fictitious. Any resemblance to actual persons, living or dead, events, or locales is purely coincidental.

ISBN: 9798776044571

2021 First Edition

Single Girl Rule #2
Girls' night is every Friday. No exceptions.

Chapter 1

MY LESSER HALF
Friday, Sept 13, 2013

"What am I going to do?" I asked. "I've been hyping up girls' night all week. And I promised Ash that it's going to be the best night of her life. But there's nothing to do here in Newark."

Teddybear stopped loofahing my thigh and looked up at me. "Permission to speak?"

I loved having my sexy bodyguard as my man servant. On any other occasion I would have made him stay silent while bathing me, but desperate times called for desperate measures. "Permission granted. But don't stop scrubbing. I'm very dirty." I winked at him.

He dropped his gaze back to my thigh. "How could you possibly be short on ideas for an epic girls' night? For the past two years you snuck away from us every chance you got. Can't you just replicate whatever you were doing those nights?"

"You want me to invite Chad to come visit from Harvard? I doubt Ash would want to spend our first girls' night being the third wheel to me and my boyfriend. And anyway - that would violate Single Girl Rule #15: No inviting guys to girls' night…unless they're strippers."

"I wasn't talking about Chad." He looked pissed that I'd even mentioned my lesser half. "I was talking about when you'd party with your friends. Other thigh, please."

I turned and put my other leg up on the little bench on the shower wall. "I don't know if that's a good idea. Those girls never liked me very much. I haven't heard from a single one of them since the day I left New York."

"Did you ever apologize for flashing all their boyfriends?"

"Why would I apologize for that? I was just trying to cheer them up. And anyway, who said you could talk?" I grabbed his head and pushed it between my thighs. *That should shut him up.*

He placed a few soft kisses against my clit as his strong hands ran up my thighs. He pushed them further apart. The force of it pushed my back up against the cold shower tiles.

"Oh God," I muttered.

He'd only been bathing me for a week, but he'd already learned what I liked.

I liked when he touched my thighs.

I liked that thing he did with his tongue.

And most of all, I liked when he took what he wanted.

This was his reward for a job well done. And I wanted him to enjoy it as much as I did. After all...it would have been insulting if he was naked in the shower with me and didn't want to fuck me.

I grabbed a fistful of his hair to make sure he wouldn't leave. But it wasn't necessary. He was going to keep devouring my pussy until I came. And then he was going to bend me over and fuck me senseless.

Ah, how I love my mornings. This was my favorite part of the day. Which got me thinking...

"Maybe this is what I should do for girls' night!"

Teddybear stopped and looked up at me.

"Don't stop. I'm just thinking out loud." I pushed his head back down. "We could do a spa night. And you and Ghost could be the spa attendants. And since you two will definitely end up stripping off your cute little spa uniforms, it wouldn't even violate rule #15."

Teddybear moved his tongue faster. Was that his way of endorsing my idea?

"You're so bad," I said. "Are you hoping I'll let you fuck my bestie?"

He shook his head and his nose brushed against my clit.

"Oh fuck," I moaned. "Yes. Just like that."

"Chastity?" said a familiar voice. A boy's voice. Chad's voice.

"Chad?" I called back. "Is that you?" *What the fuck is he doing here?!* He was supposed to be at Harvard.

"Yup! Surprise!" He paused. "Hey, when I came in here it sounded like you were talking to someone. Are you not alone in there?"

"Nope. I'm with...a friend." *Shit!*

"Oooh." Chad sounded excited. "How about I come join you?"

I laughed. "But we're naked."

"I don't mind."

"Yeah," I said. "But my friend does. How about you go wait by my room?"

"I'd rather come join."

Damn it! I should have known that telling him I was with a friend wouldn't get him to go away. He'd been begging me for a threesome all summer. But there was no way he was ready for that. He could barely please me, much less me and a friend. How embarrassing would that be for me if he couldn't get my friend off?

Teddybear, on the other hand...he could definitely handle a threesome.

Maybe he'd get one tonight.

Would Ash like that? I wasn't sure. But I had all day to figure it out.

"We're actually all done." As much as I hated to make Teddybear stop, I couldn't let him continue. Because I would definitely scream when I came. And then Chad would try to break in. And then they'd fight and it would be a whole thing. So I reluctantly pushed Teddybear's head back and pressed my finger to my lips. "Stay here until we're gone," I whispered. Then I grabbed my towel off the back of the door and slid out.

Chad was waiting in the bathroom with a big grin on his face.

"Come with me." I grabbed his hand and pulled him back to my dorm room.

Ash was off at her 8 a.m. class, so Chad and I had the room all to ourselves. Well...almost.

Ghost was waiting in the room with a delicious stack of banana pancakes, fresh from a local diner.

He bowed and handed me my utensils.

"Thank you, Ghostie," I said. "You're dismissed." I booped him on the nose and he walked out the door.

"Wow," said Chad. "You've really got Ghost trained well. I do not remember him being that agreeable."

"He and I came to an understanding. Anyway...what brings you here?"

"You."

Of course. I couldn't help but smile. "Missed me?"

"So much."

"Or did you just miss these?" I lowered my towel just enough for him to see my tits.

His eyes got a little bigger. "You know I missed those too."

I pulled my towel back up. "How's Harvard?"

"Amazing. My roommate is the son of a senator. And the guy down the hall drives a Lambo around campus. They think they have an in for some of the final clubs. Those are like the better, cooler Harvard versions of fraternities. And they're super secretive."

I stared at him. Did he think I was dumb or something? I knew what final clubs were. But it didn't hurt to stroke his ego a little. "Oooh. Secret clubs? Maybe I'll come visit when you get in and we can go to some secret parties. Want some pancakes?" I gestured to the plate that Ghost had left for me. I didn't really want to share, but it was only polite.

"I ate on the way here." He eyed me skeptically.

"Suit yourself." I stuffed a bite into my mouth. "Mmm. Delicious, pankcakey goodness."

"I thought you didn't eat carbs."

"That was the old me. The me before I broadened my horizons at this lovely institution. Now I have a theory that bread and meat go straight to my tits. What do you think?" I lowered my towel for him again.

Ash walked in and screamed. "Holy boobs!"

"Ah! You're back! Ash, meet my boyfriend, Chad. Chad, meet by bestie, Ash."

"Wait," said Ash. "Chad is *real*? I thought he was just some dude you made up as a joke."

I laughed. "Uh, no."

"But you…"

I pressed my finger to her lips. "Hush, child. I know I made him sound too good to be true. But as you can see, he's very much a real boy."

"What has she said about me?"

I hadn't really told her much about him. The only thing she knew about him was that his dick was smaller than the hot jocks'. I'd tell Chad all about my sexcapades later and he could tell me about all the hot Harvard girls he'd been getting down and dirty with. I was sure none of them were even half as hot as me, so whatevs. But I didn't want Ash spilling the beans. Especially not in the context of him having a tiny penis.

I kept my hand on Ash's mouth. "I told her that you go to Harvard. And that you're the smartest person I know. And that you're amazing in bed." I smacked Chad's ass and gave it a nice little squeeze.

"Yup," said Ash. "That's exactly what she said. Anyway, I'll let you two do whatever you two were about to do." She backed towards the door, her eyes darting back and forth between my exposed breasts and my hand on Chad's ass.

"Oh." I laughed and put my boobs away. "We weren't about to bang, if that's what you were thinking."

"Right. Okay. See ya later!"

"Wait," said Chad. "There's no reason for you to go. In fact, it'll be better if you're here to witness this."

"Witness what?" replied both me and Ash. Although Ash sounded *much* more nervous than I did. I was really starting to think she wasn't ready for a threesome either. *What am I saying?* It was so much easier for girls. And who would pass up getting pounded on both ends by two strong men?

"Well… I was sitting around with the guys and we got into this deep discussion about what we really want out of life. I mean…we're all alphas. We have the looks, the money…we can have anything. So it really just comes down to figuring out what gift we want to give to the world."

"And what gift shall you give?" I asked, trying to hide the amusement in my voice. Chad had seemed like an alpha back in high school. But now? Now I knew better.

"Myself. To you." He dropped to one knee.

Wow. I smiled to myself. I'd always thought it would be so fun to reject a proposal. But I never expected Chad to propose *this* early.

"I've spent many long nights in the wood-paneled Harvard dorms pondering my life. And I always come to the same conclusion. I want to do whatever I can to make your life amazing. So, Chastity Morgan...when we're done with college, I promise to make you the happiest woman in the world." He pulled a ring box from his pocket and snapped it open. The morning light streaming in from the window caught the diamond just so.

It was breathtaking.

But it was only two carats. Two and a half max. Which meant it was just a promise ring. Not an engagement ring. *Damn it!* So much for getting to reject his proposal.

"So what do you say?" he asked. "Will you make me the happiest man in the world?"

I shrugged and held out my ring finger. He slid the ring onto it.

"Not bad," I said. I wiggled my fingers around to make it catch the light again. Then I held it up for Ash to see.

She looked completely dumbfounded. "Congrats?"

"Thanks, bestie! Ahh! This is so exciting!"

Chad reached into his back pocket and handed me a sheet of paper. "It's about to get even better."

"What's this?" I asked.

"Read it."

I unfolded the paper. It was printed on Harvard letterhead.

Chastity Morgan,

Congratulations! You've been accepted to Harvard for the Spring 2014 semester.

I didn't bother reading the rest. Because it was exactly the same as the first acceptance letter I'd received earlier this year. The one I'd turned down. I wasn't about to waste my college years at Harvard when the guys at the University of New Castle had such bigger cocks. The rumor was true. And I was staying put.

"My roommate's dad pulled a few strings. Apparently he's friends with the dean."

"Aw, babe. It's so cute that you want me to be with you so badly."

"So is that a yes? I mean…you can finally leave this shithole and come to a real school with quality people." He looked over at Ash. "No offense."

Ash looked very much offended.

"I actually love it here," I said. I've already met some really amazing people." I walked over and threw my arm around Ash's shoulders. "And learned some life-changing stuff." *The Single Girl Rules.* If I hadn't come here, I never would have found them. And then my life would have been terrible and sad and boring. Actually, it still would have been amazing, because I'm amazing. But just like…a little less amazing. And definitely less sexy. God…when was I going to run into a man with 8 abs and 8 inches so that I could make good on Rule #8?

"You belong at Harvard with me," said Chad, waving my comment off. "It'll make networking so much easier. Everyone loves you. We'll be the ultimate power couple. No one will be able to stop us on our way to the White House."

White House? Had Chad randomly decided that he wanted to be president someday? I decided to play along. "Oooh. Yes! That'll be so fun! But I have two conditions. One, I get to wear lingerie in my official portrait. And two, we add a pool to the rose garden so that I can tan. And throw epic pool parties, of course."

"We can discuss the specifics tonight when we go out to celebrate. What's your favorite bar in town?"

"Grotto's is pretty great. But that'll have to wait. Tonight is girls' night."

"But I just drove all the way here from Harvard…"

He drove? Well, that was silly peasant behavior. He should have taken a private jet, it would have saved him loads of time. "Yeah, but Rule #2: Girls' night is every Friday. No exceptions."

"Rule #2? What are you talking about?"

Am I allowed to tell boys about the rules? I wasn't sure. I'd have to ask Slavanka if there were any footnotes or additional info to translate that might shed some light on that.

"I'll explain later. But right now, Ash and I need to get to class." I dropped my towel and pulled on some super cute leggings and a tank top. "Thanks for the ring, babe!" I gave Chad a kiss on the cheek and then grabbed Ash's hand and pulled her out of our dorm room.

"Uh…do you mind explaining to me what the hell just happened in there?" she asked.

"I'm not exactly sure, but I think Chad may have discovered cocaine. Hence the promise ring, the silly letter, and his idea of running for president." It all made sense. Tons of rich guys eventually started snorting coke. We made our way downstairs and out the door of our dorm.

"Are you sure? He seemed kind of serious about all of that… And what makes you think that's a promise ring? That really looked like a proposal to me. I'm pretty sure you just got engaged."

I held the ring up. "This little thing? An engagement ring?" The idea was laughable. "Does this look like four carats to you?"

"Yes?"

"Nope. It's only like two. Thus it's a promise ring." I held my pinky nail up to it to show how small it was.

Ash shook her head. "I don't think that's how anything works."

"Sure it is. You've heard the old saying: give her four if you want your relationship to be more."

"I've literally never heard that."

"Weird. Anyway, it's a fun little accessory. I'll have to properly thank him for it tomorrow night. Since you and I are going to be a little busy tonight." I wiggled my eyebrows at her.

She laughed. "You know you can hang out with him tonight, right? I mean, he did drive all the way down here. That must have been like a six-hour drive."

"Nonsense. We already missed girls' night last Friday because I'd just learned about the rules. There's no way I'm going to ditch you this Friday too. I have the most amazing night planned for us."

"Really?"

"Yup!" *Well, maybe.* I still had to figure out if Ash was down to bang Ghost or Teddybear. Or both. I suspected she was still jealous of what she saw at the party last Friday, even if she wouldn't admit it. The whole 'I fell asleep' thing was a total lie. She was probably just too embarrassed to say she got off to it in the closet. *Kinky bitch.* "It's going to be epic. No. Beyond epic!"

"And what exactly will we be doing?"

"It's a surprise."

"Uggh" groaned Ash. "You know I hate surprises. At least give me a hint."

"Okay. Let me think." I tapped my finger against my lips. I needed something that was spa-related. But also sex-related. *Aha!* "Cucumbers."

"No!" screamed Ash.

"What?"

"I'm afraid of cucumbers."

"How could you be afraid of cucumbers? They're like…the second-best penis-shaped fruit. Bananas are the best, obvs." And then it hit me. "WAIT!"

Ash jumped and a few passersby looked at us funny. "Wait what?"

"I just figured out what we're doing for girls' night."

"So no cucumbers?"

"No. We're not gonna have some lame spa night orgy for our very first girls' night. No, no, no. God, how did I not think of this sooner? The promise-posal. The banana pancakes. Like half of the Single Girl Rules. They've all been pointing to the same thing!"

"I have no idea what any of those things have in common."

"Oh sweet, simple Ash. We're having a bache-lorette party!"

"So Chad *did* actually propose? I'm beginning to think he shared some of that cocaine with you."

"That was a practice proposal. So now we get to have a practice bachelorette party." This was going to be so much freaking fun.

"And do you expect me to plan it?"

"My actual bachelorette party? Absolutely. And it better be amazeballs. Single Girl Rule #39: Being a maid of honor is the most sacred duty in a woman's life. But this is just a practice one, so I'll plan it. It'll be good practice for both of us."

"How are you going to plan a bachelorette party in like…12 hours?"

"One word: Banana Party."

"That's two words. And also…that doesn't sound nearly as bad as I thought it would. Because you're right - bananas are definitely the best penis-shaped fruit. Possibly the best fruit period. They're full of potassium and just all-around good for you."

Yeah they are. "Right?! Ahhh! This is going to be the best night ever!"

Chapter 2

SO MANY BANANAS
Friday, Sept 13, 2013

It had taken all day, but I'd pulled it off. Everything was set for my bachelorette party. I know, I know. Half a day feels like not enough time to plan an entire party. But in this case, it was easy. Because just like every other girl in America, I'd been planning my bachelorette party since the moment I saw my first Tommy Hilfiger men's underwear ad.

I scanned my list one more time to make sure I hadn't forgotten anything important.

Bridesmaids? *Check.*

Strippers? *Check.*

Super cute outfits? *Double check.* The outfits I'd picked out were straight fire.

An amazing venue? *Check.*

More strippers? *Check.*

"I did it," I said. I put my hand up for a high five.

"Huh?" Chad wiped his greasy pizza fingers off on his napkin and high fived me, despite looking deeply confused.

"I planned the perfect girls' night."

"For next weekend, right?"

"No, silly. For tonight. How many times do I have to tell you Rule #2: Friday night is…"

"Girls' night. No exceptions." He shook his head. "I know. But I still don't understand where these rules are coming from. Is this some sort of sorority thing?"

"Uh…" *Shit!* I'd been so busy with the party planning that I hadn't gotten a chance to ask Slavanka if there were any footnotes about keeping the rules a secret. "Yup. It's a sorority thing."

"You didn't tell me you were rushing. That's awesome! Which sorority are you going for?"

My knowledge of Greek life on campus was limited to the frat parties I'd attended. The beta boys had thrown an epic party at the dean's house. And I always walked by the Alpha Omicron house on the way to class so I could watch them working out. But sororities? I knew nothing about those. Ash and Slavanka were my sorority. Because they were the only ones who I'd shared the Single Girl Rules with. *Wait a second!* Single Girl Rules. SGR… "Sigma Gamma Rho."

Chad choked on his water. "Excuse me?"

"Sigma Gamma Rho."

"You're rushing a historically black sorority?"

Damn it! What were the odds that Sigma Gamma Rho was a real thing?! Oh well. It was too late to back down now. And I had the perfect way out. "Historically black, huh? I don't think that's accurate."

Chad typed something into his phone. And then he turned it for me to see as he scrolled through all the google images of Sigma Gamma Rho. There was not a single white girl to be found.

"Huh. I guess they are all black." I shrugged. "Honestly, I'd never noticed." I stared at him. "Oh my God, babe, are you a racist?"

"What? No." He straightened his polo shirt and looked around to make sure no one had heard my accusation. "I think it's awesome that you're rushing them. I was just surprised, that's all."

I took one more bite of pizza and then stood up. "Time for me to go meet up with the girls."

He grabbed my wrist. "Hold on. Can't I come? I promise I'll be good."

"That depends. Will you dress up in a police officer uniform and shake your cute little butt for all of us?"

"You want me to strip for all your friends?"

I nodded. "Will you do it or not?"

"I totally would, but could you imagine if a video of that leaked? My presidential bid would be finished before it even began. And anyway…I don't think your roommate could handle all this." He grabbed my hand and pushed it against his abs as he busted a move.

I wasn't sure if he was being serious or not. But if he *was* being serious…woof. His stripper moves needed some serious work. "So that's a no to the stripping then?"

"Yeah. Not happening."

"Then I guess you can't come. Rule #15: No inviting guys to girls' night…unless they're strippers."

Chad laughed and shook his head. "That can't seriously be one of the rules. But I appreciate the creativity." Then he got a serious look on his face. "Wait. You aren't gonna have strippers at girls' night, right?"

"I mean…this is my very first girls' night. And Rule #10 says that all celebrations of important life events must involve strippers. You do the math."

"Wow, these rules really focus on strippers a lot. Any other ones I should know?"

"Hmm…well, those are the only two that mention strippers explicitly. But quite a few *could* be talking about strippers. Like Rule #41: Any girl who doesn't suck a cock at the bachelorette party is uninvited to the wedding. This includes the bride. No exceptions."

"Oh, of course. Why does that even need to be a rule? Shouldn't that just go without saying?"

I could tell he was being sarcastic. But the joke was on him. Because tonight was my practice bachelorette party, and I intended to follow that rule to a T. "There's also Rule #8: If a man has 8 abs and 8 inches, he may not be refused. And let's be honest...any strippers worth hiring would fit that description."

"Oh, I like Rule #8."

"You do?" *Kinky!* I had no idea Chad liked the idea of me getting dominated by some rando with a huge cock.

"I do. Because according to that rule, girls' night is canceled and you're spending the night with me." He made a show of looking down at his package.

I burst out laughing. "What kind of math are they teaching you at Harvard? Because last time I checked, five inches is smaller than eight."

"Yeah, but no one is *actually* eight inches."

"Sure they are."

"Chastity, I've been in tons of locker rooms. And let me tell you. This right here is as big as it gets." He looked so confident.

Poor, sweet Chad. I didn't have the heart to tell him that he must be looking in all the wrong locker rooms. The Harvard badminton team wasn't exactly the pinnacle of manliness. "And I'm a very lucky girl." I held up my hand and wiggled my promise ring. "But unless you suddenly grew three inches,

then you can't invoke Rule #8. Smooches!" I blew
him a kiss, turned, and walked out of Grottos.

***

I walked into my dorm room and froze. *Holy bananas!*

"Surprise!" yelled Ash.

I just blinked. There were bananas everywhere.
Literally everywhere. Strands of bright yellow banana lights hung between the windows and our bed
posts. I was pretty sure she'd stolen them from a
monkey's luau party or something. There were yellow streamers with bananas printed on them too.
Several loaves of what appeared to be banana bread
were scattered about, presumably to ensure that one
would always be within reach. There were banana
pillows. And actual bananas were just thrown about
randomly. She'd even changed my satin sheets to
what looked like 100 thread count banana sheets.
Yes, I could tell from here. *Oh no.* That would not
do. I couldn't sleep on anything under than 1,000
thread count. I wasn't a cavewoman.

And most crazy of all was what she was wearing.
Flannel. Banana. Pajamas. *Flannel!* One of the bananas on the bed shifted and I screamed.

But it was just Slavanka in a matching set of
nightmarish flannel jammies.

"Oh, you invited Slavanka!" I said. That was the
only fun thing happening in this room right now.

"Yes. It is me. Slavanka."

I laughed. That was what I'd just said. She was so funny. I plopped myself down on my bed, ignoring the way the sheets scratched my skin. "Um…what is all this stuff, Ash?" I asked and pushed a plate of banana bread away from me.

"A Banana Party," said Ash. "I wanted to surprise you."

Poor, sweet, Ash. This is not a Banana Party. Not even in the slightest. There weren't even any monkeys. "So…this is your idea of a girls' night, huh?" Wow, had I misjudged this? This couldn't possibly be what a girls' night was. It was so…simple. The night I was planning was basically the exact opposite of this. And there would be significantly more naked men.

"Of course," Ash said. "A girls' night is eating junk food and gossiping about hot boys. Oh! And I have party games. Want to play grab-a-nana?" She pointed to a circle of rubber bananas on the floor.

Was that like grab-a-dick but with bananas? "Um…"

"Or Bananagrams?" She pulled the game out from behind her back.

I felt like a game involving spelling would be very unfair to Slavanka. What was Ash thinking?

"Or we can listen to Bananaphone!"

I just shook my head. "Banana what? I don't know what that is."

"For bananas being your favorite fruit, you sure don't know much about them." Ash turned to her computer and a horrible song started blaring. About bananaphones. I was pretty sure it was for kids. Or...pediatrists.

I shook my head because I had no idea what the fuck was happening. Had Ash and Slavanka really never heard of a legit Banana Party before? I wasn't sure why I was even asking myself that question. Because the answer was very clearly *no*.

"Oh, I almost forgot!" Ash said. "I got you a pair of pajamas so that all three of us could match!" She tossed me a pair of pajamas that unfortunately were identical to the ones she and Slavanka were wearing.

I dodged them and my elbow squished into a loaf of banana bread. *Ew.* "Ash...this is all great..." *No.* No it was not. It was horrifying. I stood up and somehow got tangled up in one of the banana streamers. "Where did you even find all this stuff?"

"At the Five and Dime on Main Street."

Was that a poor person store? I'd heard of a dime before but only when referring to a total dime of a man. I tried to remember my schooling as a youth. *Dime, dime, dime. Wait!* Did that mean 10 cents? Was all this stuff less than a dollar?

"And before you say anything, it was all heavily discounted," Ash said. "I know you love paying for stuff, but I wanted to surprise you with this. Can you even believe it? They were practically giving it away. It was my lucky day."

Yes. I could definitely believe it. "Wow."

"There's also frozen chocolate bananas in the mini-fridge. But we should eat them soon because the freezer portion of that fridge is not so great."

I was not going to eat warm bananas tonight. Unless she was using bananas as a sexy euphemism. And I was pretty sure she wasn't. But...Ash looked so freaking happy. I watched her as she pulled a banana pillow into her arms and squeezed it.

I exhaled slowly. If this was what she wanted to do... I pulled on the flannel pajama top over my clothes. Just the top. I wouldn't be caught dead in that horrible matching set.

Ash was beaming.

It wasn't the girls' night I'd imagined, but I was still with my girls. Maybe we could play grab-a-nana and get so wasted that the Bananaphone song might actually start to sound good. Wait...where is the booze?

"Strippers," said Slavanka.

Finally, someone was speaking my language. "Yes! We need strippers!" I loved Slavanka. She was such a kinky bitch.

Ash shook her head. "No. No strippers."

"No," Slavanka said. "Strippers."

"Yes," Ash agreed. "No strippers."

"No." *Long pause.* "Strippers," Slavanka said again and nodded. The word no and the nod were sending very different messages. And the pause in the middle was starting to pique my interest. Was she saying: "No, there will definitely be strippers?"

"So...yes?" I asked. "Yes to the strippers?"

"I don't know what's happening right now," Ash said. "Slavanka just said no. Come on, guys. Let's have some banana bread. And then maybe we can watch Ace Ventura. He has a pet monkey, I think. I bet there's at least one banana in that movie." She picked up the remote.

There was a knock on the door.

"Yes," Slavanka said. "I get door." She opened the door. "Yes. Strippers now."

There were too fully nude men standing in the doorway.

Slavanka, you really are a kinky bitch! She didn't even care about the stripping part. She'd just hired two nudists to come to our room. I was in love with that.

Ash screamed at the top of her lungs.

"Strippers," Slavanka said. "Bananas." She pointed to their erect penises.

Now those were my kind of bananas!

Before we could stop Ash, she ran toward the door.

Wow, she's really into this. I wondered which one she was going to attack. The guy on the left had better abs. But the one on the right looked like he had an inch on the other guy. Penis length. Not height. He was actually quite a bit shorter.

But Ash didn't jump one and start making out with him. She tried to run between them to escape.

They moved out of the way too slowly though and her hand collided with the bigger erection.

She screamed at the top of her lungs again and kept running down the hall.

Slavanka and I looked at each other.

"We should probably go after her," I said.

"Yes. Chase the silly Banana Party girl."

Yup. We both started running after Ash. But she was a speedy little thing. "I almost forgot to ask," I said to Slavanka as we ran through the green. "Are there any footnotes about sharing the rules? Like could I tell my boyfriend about them?"

"Single girl has no boyfriend."

"So…no?"

"No."

No. So the rules were only for girls' eyes. And she had a good point. Single girls didn't have boyfriends. I'd have to think about that. I wasn't sure if my relationship with Chad really counted though since he went to a different school. And the promise ring didn't mean anything. It was just a beautiful accessory with a very small diamond.

Ash sprinted across the green.

"Ash!" I yelled. "Let's just go back to the dorm!"

"No!"

Actually, that was fine. As great as the strippers looked…they were clearly amateurs. The ones I'd planned would be way better. Plus Daddy's jet was already stocked full of everything we needed. And I'd made the pilot fly all the way here. It would be a waste if we didn't use it.

I quickly sent Teddybear a text telling him and Ghost to come help me.

And then I turned around to take a selfie with Slavanka. "Single Girl Rule #7: Pics or it didn't happen!"

"Yes. Pics happen."

I snapped the perfect shot of the two of us with Ash running around behind us on the green. I snapped another and was lucky enough to perfectly capture Teddybear bagging Ash.

I spun around. My boys were just in time.

"What is this?" Slavanka asked as Teddybear lifted the bagged Ash over his shoulder.

"It's time to go." I slid my phone into my bra.

"Go to where?"

"The real Banana Party."

Chapter 3

DADDY'S FUN JET
Friday, Sept 13, 2013

"What is wrong with you?" Ash said and tore the bag off her head. The anger dissipated from her face as she looked around. "Where are we?"

"Daddy's fun jet."

"I can see that." She looked out the window. "Where are we going?"

"It's a surprise."

"No." She shook her head and turned back to me. "No, my Banana Party was a surprise. Kidnapping is not a surprise! It's a federal offense!"

Is it? That didn't sound right. "I didn't kidnap you. I offered to go back to the dorm and you said no."

"I didn't want to go back because there were naked men there!"

"Yeah. So now we're on the jet. Do you see any naked men?"

The stewardess walked by and gave me a weird look.

Girl, like you're suddenly scared of nakedness. She was naked all the time on this thing. I shot her a look back that screamed, "Don't send out the pilot naked after all." I wasn't sure she got it, but I'd figure that out later. The last thing I needed was for Ash to jump out of the jet.

I cleared my throat. "We need one more pic now that you've calmed down." I spun around and adjusted my cleavage so that it was pouring out my pajama top and then snapped a picture. Damn I looked good, even in flannel. But I looked better without it. I tore the flannel top off and stood up. "Now we go shopping."

"That's where we're going?" Ash looked relieved.

"No, silly. The shopping is coming to us." I snapped my fingers and a second stewardess pushed out a rack of clothes. I hadn't realized Slavanka would be here, but it didn't matter. Slavanka was just a little taller than Ash. Worst case scenario she'd just end up showing a little extra leg.

I walked over to the rack of clothes. Everything was perfect. Ash was going to have to wear something quite slutty unless she wanted to keep rocking those flannel PJs. I couldn't have planned this better if I'd tried.

The first stewardess came back out. "Anything else you ladies need?"

I turned to Slavanka and Ash. "Are you guys thirsty or hungry? The food is so much better than normal airplane food. You'll love it."

"I eat," Slavanka said.

"I'm actually quite parched," Ash said.

The stewardess handed them each a menu. "I'll give you some time to look it over." She walked away.

Ash's eyes bulged. "Does this say blowjob?"

"Hm?" I looked at the menu. "Oh, yeah, you can order sex stuff if you want. I figured you probably just wanted a drink though, you dirty girl."

"Why is there sex stuff on this menu?"

"Daddy likes his jets fun." Maybe Ash would be up for a naked pilot after all...

"And the stewardesses are okay with that? Isn't that like...sex slavery?"

I laughed. "They get paid. And it's not like he surprises them with it. It's part of the job description."

"Sushi served on breasts is part of the job description?" She jabbed at another line item on the menu.

"Of course. Do they not have that on coach?"

"No!"

"Well you're welcome to order it if you wanna see what it's like."

Ash laughed. "I don't think so." She looked back down at the menu. "Oooh they have banana juice? I didn't even know that was a thing. That sounds really good. Might as well stay on theme."

"Excellent choice." Banana juice was strong. She was about to have the time of her life.

"I have big sausage platter," Slavanka said. "Unless that is with the penis?"

I laughed. "No, Daddy isn't gay. It's just a tray of fine sausages. They're to die for."

"Yes. I like that."

"One banana juice, the sausage platter, and my usual!" I yelled over to the stewardess. "Now let's try some stuff on!" I tossed a slutty little dress over at Ash.

"Is this a bib?"

I looked over at her. "It's a dress."

Her eyes grew round.

"Remember, Rule #16: Either your legs, cleavage, or stomach must be showing at all times. Preferably all three."

"My ass would be hanging out," she protested.

"Hmmm, let me see." I grabbed the dress and held it up to her. "It's the perfect length. And it's nice and stretchy, so it'll be easy for you to pull it up if you need to."

"Pull it up?! For what?"

"Whatever you want, you naughty girl. You're the maid of honor at your besties' bachelorette party. No one's going to judge you."

A giant smile spread over Ash's face.

Wow, she's gonna get freaky.

"I'm your maid of honor?" she asked.

"Of course." I grabbed the maid of honor sash off the rack and put it over her head. "That's for you."

"Are you sure? I mean…I'd love to. It's just, we've only…"

I put my finger to her lips. "Hush, child. You're my bestie. And tonight we're gonna have the time of our lives. Just try not to get too much cum on your sash."

"What?!"

"Hmm, you're right. It'll be more fun if we try to get as much cum as possible on our sashes."

"No! No cum on our sashes!" Ash pulled the sash over her head. "What kind of crazy place are you taking us to?"

"Miami."

"Where in Miami?"

"Miami is best strip clubs, yes?" asked Slavanka. She took the slutty little dress from Ash. "I wear this. Stripper men will love."

"Nope. No way." Ash shook her head. "I already ran away from strippers once tonight. I don't want to have to do it again. And anyway, we're too young for strip clubs. Don't you need to be 21?"

"Only if alcohol is being served. But it's kind of a moot point when we're wearing our sashes. No one is gonna ID a bride and her bridesmaids. Especially since we're all super hot."

"So we're seriously going to a strip club? I'm not sure Chad is going to love the idea of you ogling a bunch of half-naked men all night. It would be so much better if we just turned around and went back to my Banana Party."

"Why would Chad care about strippers? He doesn't care when I use my vibrator, so why would he care if I fuck a stripper?"

"Fuck a stripper!?"

"If they're hot enough, then why not?"

"Uh…because it's cheating. And the germs. God, so many germs. And the diseases! Diseases are so much worse than germs, Chastity!"

"What kind of trashy amateur club do you think I'd take you to? Sure, there are some strippers out there who have sullied the noble profession. But real strippers all take the Strippocratic Oath. They would never harm their patrons with STDs."

"You mean the Hippocratic Oath?"

"No, silly. That's for doctors." Ash seemed so smart, but sometimes the things she said were so dumb. She really needed that banana juice ASAP to help her loosen up. Or I'd be tempted to call her a basic B, and there was no way in hell I would have a maid of honor who was a basic B.

Right on cue, the flight attendants came out with our refreshments. Slavanka barehanded a big sausage while Ash and I took big swigs of our drinks.

Slavanka was such a baller. She was going to excel tonight, I could tell.

"Wow, this is amazing!" said Ash. She took another gulp. "Can I have another of these?"

One of the flight attendants nodded and ducked back into the kitchenette.

Ash finished her first banana juice and then started on her second. "What were we talking about again?"

"Strippers," said Slavanka.

"You mean STDs," corrected Ash.

"It's probably not my place to ask this, said the flight attendant, "But what kind of horrible strippers would have STDs? You guys know to only go to clubs where they've taken the Strippocratic Oath, right?"

"That's exactly what I was saying! Thank you…" I glanced at her nametag. "…Esme."

"Okay, I'm officially lost," said Ash. "What is the Strippocratic Oath?"

"A sacred oath that all strippers have taken since the days of ancient Greece. Let me see if I can remember it…" I cleared my throat and recited:

"I swear by Dionysus, god of theater, entertainment, and festivity, and Priapus, god of the phallus, and with all the gods as my witness, that I shall uphold the following oath.

"First and foremost, I shall pleasure my patrons indiscriminately to my own enjoyment.

"I shall keep myself free of disease.

"I shall keep my patron's identities confidential, and I shall not recognize them outside of my place of work.

"I shall keep my body in peak physical condition.

"And finally, I shall use the tools and techniques of my trade to postpone my climax until my performance requires it.

"If I keep this oath, may I find eternal admiration and forever please my woman.

"And if I break this oath, may my manhood be forever giant and flaccid."

"Giant?" asked Ash. "That kind of feels like a reward for them to break the oath."

"Not for the Greeks. They appreciated the aesthetics of a tiny flaccid penis and the functionality of a monster erection. In other words...ancient Greeks loved growers. But what's really important is that line about disease. See? You have nothing to worry about."

"If that was a real oath, then maybe you'd be right. But I'm 99% sure you just made all of that up. Which was actually really impressive. Seriously…how'd you come up with all that on the spot?" Ash clumsily clapped her hands. That banana juice was hitting her hard.

"I didn't. I was reciting a real oath."

"It's legit," agreed Esme. "She got every word of it correct."

Damn right I did. I was starting to like this Esme chick. Daddy really knew how to pick 'em.

"I'll tell you correct words," said Ash.

Um…what? I held back a laugh. Seriously, was she drunk already? She'd only had a glass and a half of the good stuff.

"Esme can take my sash and go to the strip club in my place," Ash said. "And I'll stay back to make sure no one steals our jet. There's more banana juice, right?" She downed her second glass and handed it to Esme. "More please."

"You're my maid of honor. You can't ditch me."

"Sure I can."

"Then you're uninvited to the wedding."

"There is no wedding, so that's fine." Ash started on her third glass of banana juice.

Damn it! She had a good point. But luckily I knew her weakness. "How about this. You and I will play a classic bachelorette party game. Winner gets to choose if we go to Miami or if we turn around and go back to your Banana Party."

Ash looked so excited. "And there won't be any more surprise strippers at my Banana Party?"

I turned to Slavanka.

She shook her head. "No more strippers. I only buy them for thirty minute. I hate waste money. We waste money since we run."

I turned back to Ash. "There you have it. No more strippers at the Banana Party. Do we have a deal?"

"I would say yes, but I forgot to bring Banana-grams. So I guess we have to turn around to go get it."

"That is not a classic bachelorette party game."

"Then no deal."

"Okay. Esme, would you please tell the pilot to put the plane on autopilot and begin our special show?"

"What?" asked Ash. "What's his special show?"

I wiggled my eyebrows. There was no special show planned. As much as I loved joking around about our pilot stripping for us…unfortunately he was like…60 years old. And definitely not hot. But Ash didn't have to know that. "You'll see."

"No! Fine. We can play your game."

"And the winner gets to decide what we do?"

Ash let out a long sigh. "Yes."

We pinkie-shook on it. "Alright. Game time." Poor Ash didn't stand a chance. I opened the cabinet and pulled out my all-time favorite game.

"What the hell is that?" asked Ash. "Is that two dildos?"

Kind of. "You've never played Pump Race?"

"No."

"That's okay. It's super simple to play." I suction-cupped the game to the table and poured water into the reservoir in the middle. "You just pump as fast as you can, and whoever gets squirted in the face first wins."

"So it's a handjob race?" asked Ash.

"Exactly!" I took a seat on my side of the table and gestured for Ash to sit across from me. "Ready to lose?"

"I nominate Slavanka as my champion," said Ash.

Slavanka ripped off half a sausage with her teeth and then put her sausage platter aside. "I give handjob to strange plastic toy."

"What?" I asked. "This isn't a medieval trial by combat. You can't nominate a champion."

"Gah, fine." Ash polished off her third glass of banana juice and took a seat.

I double-checked to make sure the game was set to hard mode - that way Ash couldn't win with a few lucky pumps - and then stretched my wrist out. I didn't want to injure myself before the real handjobs started.

"May the best woman win," I said. "Slavanka, you tell us when to begin."

"Yes," said Slavanka.

"Does that mean go? Or not?"

"Yes."

"Which one?" I asked.

"No."

"What?"

"Yes."

"Just go!" yelled Esme.

Ash's hand shot out and started pumping way faster than I had anticipated. But I wasn't worried. At least…I wasn't worried at first. But then Ash really started getting into it.

Not only did she have a perfect rhythm, but she was applying a nice circular motion each time she pumped up. She was a freaking natural at giving handjobs. *#Respect.*

"Getting tired?" I asked after we'd been pumping for at least two minutes. Hard mode was no joke.

Ash laughed. "No way. You?"

"Not a chance." We both started pumping faster. There was no way I was going to lose this. I had so much freaking practice. Way more than Ash.

But then Ash leaned forward and started sucking on it.

"Damn!" yelled Esme. "You go girl!"

Ash started gagging on it, but that didn't stop her. She was sucking like a champ.

It was a shame, though, because I never lost. A few more pumps and…

Ash pulled back from her dildo and water spilled from her mouth. She giggled and turned away as the dildo shot more water into her face.

I stared at her in shock. *Holy shit.* Girl had game.

"Boom!" she yelled. "You lose, sucker!"

"Best out of three?"

"No way. I won fair and square. Which means I choose where we go next."

"Should I have the pilot turn around?" asked Esme.

"Hell no," said Ash. "My bestie is getting married, and it's my job to make sure she has the best night of her life! Onward to Miami!" She threw her hands in the air.

Wait, what?

"Slavanka, give me my dress back. And Esme, bring us all more banana juice!" She hoisted her empty glass into the air. "Best. Night. EVER!"

And suddenly everything made sense. The banana juice had worked its magic and turned cute, nervous Ash into wild, party girl Ash. And I was loving it.

She stripped off her banana pajamas and slid into the slutty little dress.

"Oh my God," she said. "My ass looks freaking amazing in this." She clapped her hands over her mouth. "Oh no! Does it look *too* good? I don't want to look better than the bride. That would be so rude."

"You're fine, Ash." She was hot, but there was only one Chastity. *Moi.* I tore off my pajamas and started trying on dresses.

"Slavanka, get over here and try some stuff on!" said Ash. "And you two!" She pointed at Esme and the other flight attendant. "You're coming too."

"Really?" they asked.

"Yup," I said. I knew they rarely got to leave the plane because Daddy went hard. #GetHardPartyHard. It was a boy thing. "You guys have to come. I'd look so lame with only two bridesmaids. I need a whole squad." I tossed them each a bridesmaid sash and rifled through the dresses on the rack. I needed to find something amazing.

Thirty minutes later, we all looked hot as hell. My four girls were rocking pink mini-dresses with white sashes. But I was gonna get all the stares.

Cleavage? Check.

Tummy? Not a ton showing, but my dress did have a sexy little cut-out.

Legs? Those were the showstopper. My special order Odegaard gladiator boots were giving me life, and they even had a matching white bridal garter.

They. Were. Everything. I was definitely gonna get railed tonight.

I made a mental note to do more custom orders for Odegaards - especially with 12 hour turnaround times for only $100K - and then snapped a selfie of us as the plane rolled to a stop in the terminal.

"Welcome to Miami, ladies," said the pilot over the intercom. "It's currently 82 degrees with a chance of thunderstorms in the forecast. I hope you enjoy the rest of your evening."

A little humidity never stopped me. Miami was my bitch!

Esme opened the door and warm, humid air flooded into the plane. But what really got my attention was who was standing on the tarmac.

"Damn it!" I said. "What are *you* doing here?"

Chapter 4

ASH'S WORST NIGHTMARE
Friday, Sept 13, 2013

Ghost narrowed his eyes. "We need to talk."

"We do," I agreed. "Your suit is a mess. You look like you just came out of a tumble cycle. You should really keep your suits in better condition." I strutted down the stairs of my private jet and straightened his lapel.

He growled.

"Why are you here? I told you - no boys allowed at my bachelorette party. So unless you've taken the Strippocratic Oath…"

"You're in danger."

"Ooooh. What kind of danger?" I bit my lip. I hoped he was about to have his way with me. I loved when Ghost lost control. "Do tell. Is a kidnapper after me?"

"Yes."

I put my hands to my face in mock surprise. "Oh no! Not a kidnapper! Is he going to take me and make me suck his big cock?"

"This isn't a fucking joke. If it was, I wouldn't have just spent an hour getting bounced around that damned cargo hold."

Ah, so that's why your suit is so sloppy looking. "Aww, Ghostie. I knew you loved me." I gave him a big kiss on the cheek. *Ow, stubble much?* He could learn a thing or two from Teddybear. Teddybear knew I liked my men clean-shaven.

"I'm just doing my job."

"Oh really? Because it kind of just seems like you're jealous that you won't be the guy who gets to ruin my bomb-ass bachelorette makeup with a thick cumshot. But don't worry...this make-up is legit. It'll take a massive cumshot to fully ruin it." *Like the ones you deliver, you naughty boy.*

He growled again.

"Tell you what. Why don't you wait on the plane for me? If none of the strippers are hot enough, I'll let you do the honors." The odds of that happening were almost 0. But it didn't hurt to have a backup plan.

"You're not going anywhere."

"Yes I am. Or have you forgotten about the little video we made?"

He reached into his jacket pocket and handed me a grainy photo of a Samoan shoulder tatt. "This is Luigi Locatelli's enforcer. I have good intel that he's here in Miami. Good luck not getting kidnapped by him tonight." He slapped the picture onto my chest and turned to walk away.

To anyone standing on the tarmac he must have looked so hot strutting his stuff. Which gave me an idea…

"Wait!" I called.

He stopped and turned back.

I tossed him my phone.

"We need a slow-mo video of us getting off the plane." I ran back up the stairs. "Come on, girls!" I waved back into the plane for them to come join me.

"I probably didn't hear this right, but did he say something about us getting kidnapped?" asked Ash.

"Oh, you know Ghost. He's just being a drama queen." I flipped my hair and strutted down the stairs again. This time trying to make Ghost drool. *What? Sue me.* I had a thing for Ghost. I wanted him to growl my name while pounding me from behind.

I got it perfect on the very first take, but *someone* - *cough* Ash *cough* - totally flubbed it. It was like she had never walked in heels before. So I had her swap her 6" heels out for some flats. Take two was better. But still not perfect. Take three was perfection.

"Thanks, Ghostie!" I said. I stood on my tiptoes and gave him a kiss on the cheek. "Now go wait on the plane like a good boy." I slapped his ass and shooed him off.

And then the sky *opened up*.

"Ahhh!" I screamed. "Ghostie! Save us!"

He just grunted and walked off. But somehow the rain never touched my head. Or any of my bridesmaids.

I looked around in confusion.

Was this a bachelorette party miracle? The work of God?!

No. It was the work of Teddybear.

He'd come out of nowhere with two umbrellas and saved us from getting absolutely drenched.

"Teddybear! My savior!"

He smiled down at me.

"Get us to Club Ice without any of us getting a drop of rain on our dresses, and I'll give you a special surprise next week."

He nodded and walked us over to a limo.

Fifteen minutes later we were at Club Ice. Teddybear once again held umbrellas over us as we walked to the entrance of the club. The rain dripping off the ice-like façade created a cool melting effect.

"Don't we have to wait in line?" asked Ash, pointing to the massive line wrapping all the way around the building.

"Watch and learn." I strutted right up to the bouncer. But he moved to block our path.

"ID please," he said.

"It's my bachelorette party." I pointed half at my bride-to-be sash and half at my breasts.

"I still have to make sure you're 21."

What the hell? It was annoying, but I'd planned for it. I reached into my clutch and pulled out a fake ID for each of us. "Here you go."

He took them and squinted. And then he disappeared into the club.

"What'd you just give him?" asked Ash.

"Our IDs."

"But…my ID is in my clutch." She pulled it out and waved it around.

"Put that away! I gave him our *other* IDs."

"Other IDs? Like passports?"

"No," said Slavanka. "Chastity use fake documents. Illegal. And sexy."

Ash's eyes got huge. "Fake IDs?! Are you trying to get us thrown in jail?"

"No. Be cool. I bet he just went inside to make sure the VIP lounge is ready for us. Why are you so wet, by the way? Did Teddybear forget to cover you?"

Ash mumbled something.

"What was that?" I asked.

"It's sweat," she said a little louder. "Lying makes me nervous."

"We're not lying. We're getting into the hottest club in the city. If it makes you feel better, it's not even a strip club."

"Really?" She looked a little relieved.

Which was weird. She needed more banana juice ASAP.

"Really." I motioned to all the douchy guys lined up. "Do those guys look like they'd be waiting in line to see a bunch of male strippers?"

"No."

"He does," said Slavanka, brazenly pointing at a guy in a *very* nice pair of loafers.

"True."

The bouncer returned and handed me our IDs. "Welcome to Club Ice. It's our pleasure to host your bachelorette party this evening. The VIP lounge is the first door on the right."

"Told ya," I said to Ash. I linked my arm through hers and pulled her into the club.

My whole bride squad followed me down the hall to the VIP lounge.

The door slammed shut behind us.

"Why's it so dark in here?" asked Ash.

That was a good question. I was used to mood lighting in fancy clubs, but this was a bit extreme. I used the light on my phone to locate a light switch.

But when I flipped it on…something seemed very wrong.

"Oh fuck," I muttered. Because this wasn't like any VIP lounge I'd been in before. The wooden benches and metal bars had more of a jail cell vibe. I thought back to my plans for the night and nodded.

Actually, this seemed just about right. We were right on time.

"Sex gulag?" asked Slavanka. "Or real arrest?"

Ash started fanning her armpits. "I never thought I'd say this, but I hope you lured me into a sex dungeon."

I decided that leaning into the fake arrest thing would be the most fun for everyone. It would be so unexpected when we arrived at our final destination. I pretended to try to open the door that we'd just come through, but it didn't budge. "Oh no," I said. "Yelp didn't say anything about sex dungeons, so I'd say we got busted for those fake IDs."

"No. No!" Ash was pacing so fast. "This can't be happening! I'm not built for prison."

"Chill, girl. No one is going to prison. Single Girl Rule #29…"

"Every girl deserves a big cock on her birthday," said Slavanka.

"What?" asked Ash. "How does that apply?"

"We no get big cock in lady prison. So sad." Slavanka slumped down on a wooden bench.

"That's Rule #38," I corrected. "Rule #29 is single girls don't get speeding tickets."

Ash shook her head. "Flashing your boobs might work to get out of a little speeding ticket, but using a fake ID is a way bigger deal. Is it a felony? What if it's a felony?"

"Then I'll call Daddy and have him fix it," I lied. Daddy could not know about this. He'd be angry with me. I wasn't supposed to go out on weekends anymore. Or was it weeknights? Maybe it was all of them... "Or I could just blow the cop. Hmm...yeah, that sounds more fun."

"What if there's more than one?" asked Ash. "Cops usually travel in twos."

"This is ridiculous," Esme said. "I'm over 21. Besides, there are five of us. We could take care of the entire station if we had to."

Shhh, don't give away the surprise! I gave Esme a high five. "Yeah we could! See, Ash? It'll be fine."

A door on the other side of the room opened and two cops stepped through. They were both well over 6 feet and absolutely *rocking* their uniforms. If I didn't know better, I would have thought they were strippers dressed as cops. Which totes made sense.

"Good evening, ladies," said the hotter cop. His badge said King on it.

"Hello, officer," I said. "How can we help you?"

"Well," said Officer King. "We got a call about some girls using fake IDs. Any idea why we might have gotten a call like that?"

"No clue," said Esme. "There must be some sort of mix-up. We're all legal." She pulled out an ID and held it through the bars.

The other officer - Officer Grant - grabbed it. He shined a light on it and flipped it over. "It's legit," he said eventually.

Of course her ID was legit. Esme and the other flight attendant were well into their twenties. Unlike us college freshmen. Was it already time for sexual favors? According to my itinerary the real fun didn't start for another hour or so.

Officer King said something, but I didn't really hear it. I was too busy picturing how nice it would be to sit on his beautiful face. He had perfect lips. Not too big and not too thin. And that smile... *Yum.*

"Well?" he asked, staring at me.

"Yes, Officer?"

"I asked to see your ID."

"Oh, right. No problem." I pulled my dress down and shook my tits at him. "How's that?"

The corner of his mouth ticked up a little. He hit a button on the wall and there was a loud buzz and a click. Officer Grant slid our cell open.

That's right. The girls work every time! Especially after my new diet of meat and bread. They were better than ever.

"Thanks, boys," I said. "Just let us know if there's anything else we can help you with."

Officer King grabbed my arm as I passed.

God he's strong. His fingers were just rough enough. And the scar on the back of his hand showed he was a real man.

"Where do you think you're going?" he asked.

"To party my face off, clearly. Wanna join?"

"Hmm, try again."

"To… To jail?" stuttered Ash.

"Bingo," said Officer King as he slapped some cuffs on me.

God, I loved being handcuffed. I just wished he'd tighten them a little more. Soon I'd be screaming his name as the metal bit into my skin. I gave him my sauciest wink.

They cuffed the rest of my girls and led us out to their SUV. They piled us all into the back and sped off.

"I officially hate you," said Ash.

I patted her leg. "It'll be fine. They probably just want to show us off to all the other guys at the station." Ash was so gullible. I couldn't wait to see her expression when she saw our final destination.

"Are you sure? Because it really seems like we just got arrested for real."

"Na. They didn't read us our rights or anything. This isn't a legit arrest."

"Oh my God." Ash went even paler than usual. "Oh God. Oh God. What did Ghost say to you about that kidnapper when we got off the plane?"

"Just some silliness about Daddy's rival's enforcer being in Miami tonight. But he was definitely just looking for an excuse to have us not go out tonight. Ghost hates fun."

"What if those officers didn't read us our rights because they aren't actually officers? What if they're the kidnappers?" Ash hissed.

"Then I hope they treat me the way Ghost said they would." I fanned myself thinking about being double-teamed by those hot cops.

"Chastity!" whisper-yelled Ash. "This isn't a joke! And why are the windows blacked out? Is that normal for a cop car?"

"Huh." I pressed my face to glass but I couldn't see a thing. "No, that's not normal." This was so much more sexual than a normal cop car. And it probably cost four times as much. Hadn't Ash ever seen the back of a gross cop car before?

"They take us to sex gulag?" asked Slavanka with a big smile.

"Worse," whispered Ash in the most dramatic way possible.

"Oh, come on. There's only a very small chance that we just got kidnapped. But if we did, it's gonna make for the most epic bachelorette party story ever."

"That would be pretty epic," added Esme. "For what it's worth, Zoraida and I are both black belts.

So if those hot cops are kidnappers, then they're about to get their asses kicked."

The other flight attendant, Zoraida, nodded.

"Damn," I said, nodding at the two flight attendants. "Daddy really did a good job picking you two. It's an honor to call you my bridesmaids."

The car screeched to a halt. The door opened a second later. And based on the cruisers parked next to us and the boring architecture of the building, we were definitely at the fake police station.

They led us inside and put us in a holding cell.

Officer King held out a plastic tray. "Cell phones, please."

#*Lame!* I hated places that didn't allow pictures. Didn't they know about Single Girl Rule #7: Pics or it didn't happen? We all pulled out our phones and put them in. But luckily I still had my backup phone.

"Thank you, ladies. Please sit tight for just a moment while I grab some paperwork." He left us alone in the cell.

Ash spent the next ten minutes trying to figure out what kind of paperwork he was gonna bring us. Her theory was that he was gonna split us all up into interrogation rooms and hit us with phonebooks until we ratted each other out.

The door clicked open and Officer King walked in carrying five stacks of papers.

"Sign these releases and present them to the attendant at the end of the hall. Enjoy your evening."

He handed us each a stack and left through a secret door in the back of our cell, leaving the door wide open behind him.

I glanced down at the top sheet of paper. RELEASE FORM was at the top in big bold letters. I scanned it and it was exactly what I'd expected, so I signed the last page and stood up. This was going to be so much fun.

"Ready to go, girls?" I asked.

"I'm so confused," said Ash.

"Just sign it. Page 15."

"Is it a confession?"

"No. It's a release form."

"Oh, thank goodness. So we aren't being charged for using fake IDs and then trying to seduce Officer King?"

"Nope."

She let out a *huge* sigh. "Well shit, then let's sign and get the hell out of here before they change their minds." She flipped to the back and signed.

"I sign," said Slavanka.

"Think your father will be okay with this?" asked Esme.

I nodded. "For sure. If he gives you any shit about it, just say I made you do it."

She shrugged and they both signed too.

We took the signed papers and left our cell through the secret door.

This hallway was much different than the one we'd entered in. That one had been all linoleum and cheap tan walls and fluorescent lights. But this hallway…this was luxurious. It was all white marble and columns and candlelight.

"What the hell is happening?" asked Ash. "Did we get kidnapped after all? Because this hallway is definitely giving me drug lord mansion vibes. I prefer police station vibes over this."

Ew, really? This was so much better. I needed to teach Ash a thing or two about high-end interior decorating. "No idea," I lied as we turned a corner. We were finally here.

A woman in a tuxedo - complete with fancy white gloves - stopped us in front of two massive wooden doors.

"Papers, please," she said.

I handed her the stack.

"Thank you very much." She opened the doors and gestured for us to go through, bowing slightly in the process. "It's my distinct pleasure to welcome you ladies to the Banana Party."

Chapter 5

THE (REAL) BANANA PARTY
Friday, Sept 13, 2013

"I'm so confused," said Ash as we stepped onto a lavish elevator lined with mirrors.

"Me too," I agreed. "I thought for sure Officer King was gonna strip for us. He was giving me some serious big dick energy." I fanned myself just thinking about him in that uniform.

"No, not that. I was talking about the fake IDs. And getting arrested. And then our jail cell having a secret door that led to a hallway that led to some random lady welcoming us to the Banana Party." Then recognition flashed across her face. "Wait a second. You planned all of this!"

"Of course I planned this, girl. I told you we were gonna go to the Banana Party for my bachelorette party."

"What the hell, Chastity! I was totally freaking out thinking that we legit got arrested! You should have told me it was all part of the plan."

"I thought everyone knew that you could only get to the Banana Party by looking super hot and using a fake ID to get into some lame club."

"Why would I know that?" asked Ash. She looked to her fellow bridesmaids. "Did you guys know that?"

"I'd heard rumors," said Esme. Zoraida nodded in agreement.

"Handsome officer take us to sex gulag," added Slavanka. "Yes, yes."

"Are there any other surprises I should know about?" asked Ash. "Oh God, is some naked dude gonna attack us the second we step off this elevator?" She jammed her elbow against the bottom button labeled JAIL. The only other option was ROOF, which appeared to be where we were headed. The JAIL button lit up, but we continued going up. Because that was how elevators worked. You couldn't just switch directions all willy-nilly.

Damn, being fake-arrested really sobered Ash up quick. She needed more banana juice immediately. "Ash, don't be ridiculous. Single Girl Rule #15: No inviting guys to girls' night." I probably should have mentioned the second part of Rule #15 - *...unless they're strippers* - but I didn't want to spoil the surprise. Or for her to run away. "It's almost a shame that there aren't gonna be any boys there, though. Because if there were, they'd definitely want to bang us." I pointed to myself in the mirror. *God I look hot tonight.*

"Ah!" screamed Ash. "What am I wearing?!" She tugged on the hem of her very sexy pink dress.

"The dress you chose…"

"Nope. I would not have chosen this dress. It's way too short. And I would never wear pink. It looks horrible with my hair."

That much was true. Even though I'd primarily planned tonight to help Ash have the time of her life, this was still a mock-bachelorette party. And I took every part of that very seriously, including practicing being a bridezilla. I wanted to say something sassy AF. But this didn't seem like the best time to tell her that the pink clashed terribly with her hair. She was already spiraling.

"You look amazing," I said, holding back my desire to be a bridezilla. *Other than the pink.*

"God, I need to change immediately." She tugged on the hem again.

But I wasn't paying attention to her anymore, because the elevator had just opened onto the roof deck of one of the tallest buildings in Miami.

"Ahhh! I squealed. "I can't believe we're at a real Banana Party! Let's do this." I hooked arms with Ash and Slavanka and pulled them off the elevator into what looked like a jungle.

But Ash wouldn't budge.

"Ash, what are you doing?" I asked.

She crossed her arms in front of her chest. "I'm not getting off this elevator."

"Why? Because of the dress? Or because you're scared some stripper is gonna mollywhop you the second you get off?"

Her eyes grew round. "Well I wasn't scared of that second thing, but now I kind of am."

I laughed. "Ash, come on. The Banana Party is only for girls. No boys allowed." *Luckily strippers don't count as boys.*

"Okay…" She tentatively stepped forward. And then she looked around with a frown on her face. "This is it?" she asked. She sounded completely unimpressed.

"What do you mean *this is it*?" I motioned to the thick, twisted tree trunks all around us. And their bright green leaves. If not for the neon green lights draped between the trees like vines and the sky-scrapers just visible through the thick canopy, I would have thought we were actually in a jungle.

The rain from earlier had been replaced by clear skies, and a gentle ocean breeze brought a slight chill to the air. Which was perfect, because Ash was already drenched in sweat.

"Sure, it's a neat jungle," said Ash. "But it's not supposed to be a jungle party. It's a Banana Party. And I don't see any bananas. I had so many actual bananas at my Banana Party." The distant howl of a monkey made her jump and hide behind me. "Holy shit! What the hell was that?"

"Monkey," said Slavanka.

"Relax," I said. "They won't attack us. Unless we want them to." I winked at her.

She laughed. And then she frowned. "Wait, what was that wink for? Are monkeys seriously going to attack us?"

"You'll see," I said with another wink. "Come on…we should hurry. I don't want to be late and miss out on getting a good table." I brushed a few low-hanging branches out of our way and pulled Ash along the tiled path through the jungle. We soon came to a big clearing with a dance floor, a stage, and three tiers of seating.

I pointed to an empty table front and center, right by the dance floor. "There. That's our table!"

We rushed across the dance floor to the table. But *just* before we got there, a group of five girls snaked it from us.

"Excuse me," I said to one of them. "But this is my table."

"Says who?"

Excuse me? "It's my bachelorette party." I went to sit down but she pulled the chair away from me.

"Oh my God," said the girl. "Congratulations! But it's also my bestie's 21st birthday. And she really wants this table too." She blew up two giant "21" balloons and tied them to a chair to claim their territory.

What the hell? For a second I was pissed that some birthday girl was trying to steal my spotlight. This was supposed to be *my* Banana Party. Not some joint venture. But then I realized that I'm me. And I'm amazing. No one could steal the spotlight from me, no matter how hard they tried. It was best if I just ignored their existence.

And honestly, this wasn't even the best table. The table right above it on the second tier was way better. It was closer to the bar, and it had a way better view of the stage. Ash would appreciate both of those things. That girl desperately needed more banana juice. And the stage…well, it would be a disaster to not have a good view of the stage at a Banana Party.

"Awww, happy birthday," I said to the one I assumed was the birthday girl. But who could really be sure which one it was with their complete lack of proper accessorizing? No sashes. No tiaras. And no matching outfits. If not for their admittedly impressive make-up, I might have mistaken them for a roving band of homeless dudes. "Come on, girls. Let's go get a better table." I flipped my hair and my amazingly dressed squad followed me up the stairs to our table.

"Where's all the banana bread?" asked Ash when we sat down. "The stress of getting fake-arrested has me famished."

"I don't think they have any," I said. Most of the girls here were probably too dense to know that the secret to big tits was bread. I remembered when I used to be basic and didn't eat carbs. "But I bet they do have some banana juice."

"Oooh! Yes!"

We got up and headed to the bar.

"Two banana juices, please."

"Slushy or liquid?" asked the girl behind the bar.

I looked at Ash.

"Slushy," she said. "That sounds so freaking good."

"I'll have the same."

The bartender filled two glasses from a slushy machine and walked over to a penis-shaped ice luge. "Who's going first?"

"Me!"

I got on my knees and opened my mouth as she poured my slushy into the top of the sculpture. I caught as much as I could in my mouth, but some spilled onto my chin. "Oops." I wiped it off as sexily as possible. If there had been any boys around, they totally would have wanted to add to the mess. But alas...the Banana Party had just begun. "Your turn."

Ash's eyes were huge.

"Oh come on, it'll be good practice for later."

Her eyes got even bigger.

"I'm joking." And then I realized she wasn't actually looking at me. "What are you looking at?"

She pointed behind me.

I spun around, but she was just pointing at some trees. "I don't see anything."

"You missed it. There was someone hiding behind those trees watching you drink your slushy. I think it was a monkey."

Yes! I knew exactly what it was. And Ash would find out soon enough. "Well of course it was a monkey. Monkeys love bananas."

"But there aren't any bananas here. Unlike my Banana Party. I really think we should have just stayed back at the dorm and played Bananagrams."

"There most certainly *are* bananas here." I pointed at a bushel of bananas hanging from a tree.

"Those are neon yellow lights shaped like bananas."

"Yeah, but a monkey wouldn't know that. Now are you gonna drink your slushy or not?"

She shook her head.

"Then no slushy for you," said the bartender. "Slushies are only for the ice luge."

"Really?"

The bartender nodded. "You can have a glass of banana juice, though."

"Fine," said Ash.

"Make it ten," I added.

"Ten?" asked Ash. "I like banana juice, but I don't need that much."

"For the table." *Kind of.* Honestly I kind of hoped Ash would drink all ten. Or at the very least three, since that was apparently how many it took to get her to start sucking on penis-shaped objects.

We grabbed the two trays of drinks and went back to the table.

Ash downed her entire banana juice the second we sat down.

There we go.

"God this stuff is so good," she said. "I can't believe I never knew about it until tonight." She took another swig. "Oh, look! Someone's on stage!"

A girl in a safari outfit tapped on a mic a few times.

"G'day, babes. Welcome to the Banana Party!" she said in an Australian accent.

"Wahoo!" I cheered along with at least thirty other girls. Maybe forty. This was a big ass Banana Party.

"Before we begin, there are two simple rules. First, touch the wildlife at your own risk. And second...do not, under any circumstances, ring this gong." She pointed at a big gong in the center of the stage. "If you fail to follow these rules, Banana Party LLC is not liable for whatever might happen. Any questions?" She didn't wait for anyone to answer. "Great!"

Oooh! I knew exactly what the first warning meant. But I'd never heard of a forbidden gong at a Banana Party. My mind started running wild with all the sexy punishments I could receive for hitting that gong. I was 100% going to hit it now. How could I not? I loved doing things I wasn't supposed to do.

"Our signature banana splits will be served later in the evening," she continued. "You can place your orders now using the tablets at each table." She walked over to the DJ booth and put one headphone to her ear. "Finally, let me remind you that this is a ladies only event, and your phones have all been taken for safe keeping... So what happens at the Banana Party stays at the Banana Party. Now let's dance!!!"

Music started blaring through the speakers as girls rushed to the dance floor.

"Banana splits?!" yelled Ash. "Yes! I freaking love bananas." She picked up a tablet and it slipped out of her hands, but she didn't seem to notice. "And I love you. All of you." She waved around the table. "You're my ride or die bitches."

Wow. That banana juice really hits her fast.

"Do you think she's okay to have more banana juice?" I whispered to Esme.

"If they're full strength, probably not. I had a feeling she wasn't gonna handle her liquor well so I tried to water them down some. But she was downing those things. She probably had the equivalent of two full drinks on the plane."

And she'd already downed one here. Which meant this was her fourth. I tried to take it from her, but she pulled it out of my reach.

"Hey! Get your own!"

Gladly. I took a big gulp of banana juice. I could see why she loved it so much. Of all the alcohol I'd had, it went down the smoothest. Hardly burned at all.

"These banana splits are gonna be epic," said Ash. "Did I mention how much I love bananas? Ooooh! What kind are you gonna order?"

"Hmm…" I picked up my tablet and looked at the options.

"I'm getting an extra-large double with hot fudge and nuts," Ash said. "And for my ice cream…ew. Why do they have olive and ginger as options? I'm just gonna go with extra extra dark chocolate. Oh! And definitely the secret sauce."

Wow. It was extremely tempting to just let her roll with that order. But I wanted her to ease into the fun.

"Can I see that for a sec?" I asked.

"Sure." She handed me the tablet. "You know, I think I might have been a little quick to judge this Banana Party." She downed a little more banana juice. "I'm still disappointed by the lack of banana bread, but this epic banana split might just make up for it."

"Mhm," I said, not really listening. I was too busy fixing her order to be something more manageable. I switched double to single, XL to medium, extra extra dark chocolate to vanilla, and got rid of the special sauce. Then I hit order.

And then I copied her original order onto my tablet. What can I say? She had good taste, even if she didn't realize what she was ordering.

"We dance now?" asked Slavanka.

"Yeah!" screamed Ash. "I LOVE THIS SONG!" *Get Low* had just started playing.

"Right?" I yelled over the music. "This is my jam!"

We all stood up. Slavanka pulled her straps off her shoulder and let her tits spill out.

"Slavanka!" yelled Ash. "Your tits are amazing! I just wanna…" She mimed motorboating Slavanka.

Wow. Ash was so drunk. And apparently drunk Ash just loved everything. Even Slavanka's tits.

"Wait," said Ash. "Why are your tits out? Should mine be out too?" She reached up to her straps.

"This bachelorette party, yes?" asked Slavanka.

I nodded, but even I was confused about this. Slavanka really was a dirty little ho, and I was here for it.

Slavanka nodded too. "We take clothes off now."

"Is that what they do in Russia?" I asked. I loved learning about new cultures.

"Bride and friends make sex with all village boys. When boys arrive?"

"I wish there were boys," Ash said. "God, I love boys. But that stupid DJ said no boys allowed." She gave the DJ a thumbs down and blew a raspberry at her. "Just kidding," she yelled. "You're amazing!"

Slavanka frowned and pulled her dress back up over her breasts. "Americans strange."

Be patient, you kinky bitch.

Chapter 6

BANANA SPLITS
Friday, Sept 13, 2013

I struck poses to the beat of the music as my bridesmaids pretended to take paparazzi photos of me. I shimmied and blew a kiss at Slavanka and she pretended to be knocked down by the sexiness of it.

I laughed as Esme caught her before she actually fell on the dance floor. And then I slapped Ash's ass as she gulped down more banana juice.

Crap, where'd she find another glass of banana juice? I kept trying to corral them away from her. But drunk Ash was speedy as hell.

Ash started jumping up and down, throwing her hands in the air. She was by far the worst dancer. But she was having the time of her life. I could tell.

Esme and Zoraida were so good at dancing, but the real star was Slavanka. I'd never seen such an elegant fusion of classical ballet and twerking. If there had been any men here, they would have been all over her. As soon as they were done with me, that is. Because even though her ballet twerking was hot, my dancing was clearly superior.

I dipped it low and grabbed Ash's hips to try to help her with her rhythm. It did not work. Each time I tried to shift her hips left, she'd thrust forward. Was her only dancing experience watching male strippers or something?

"I love bananas!" yelled Ash, spilling some of her drink on the floor.

"Yeah!!!" *Wait…where'd she get another banana juice?* She now had one in each hand. I tried to grab one from her, but she spun around and then took a big sip from each. Then she handed them to some random girl, slapped her own ass, and started doing the thrusting thing again.

I couldn't help but laugh.

"Babes!" said the DJ over the loudspeaker. "Please return to your tables. It's time for dessert!"

"YES!" screamed Ash. "Come on! Let's go eat our banana splits!" She grabbed my arm and pulled me off the dance floor. But she didn't have to. This was the part of the night I'd been waiting for.

I pulled out my backup phone and checked my makeup in the mirror app. Flawless, obvs. Just like I'd told Ghostie - only a massive cumshot could ruin my makeup. And I had not taken one of those tonight. *Yet.*

The lights dimmed and a monkey howled. But this time it sounded *much* closer than before.

Everyone looked around. Especially Ash. She looked so excited.

And I couldn't blame her one bit. I could hardly contain my excitement either. I took a second to make sure my tits looked perfect in my dress.

Here we go.

The music switched to a tribal beat.

A spotlight lit up the stage.

And a man burst through the curtain. He danced to the music while also somehow balancing a carved wooden cloche with one hand.

Oh, and he was dressed in a monkey costume. Complete with a big grinning monkey mask.

"That's him!" gasped Ash. "The monkey who was watching us!"

Maybe. It wasn't like there was only one monkey at a Banana Party. How did Ash not know that? Her lack of knowledge of what happened at Banana Parties was quite shocking.

I sat back in my chair and drank in the whole performance.

The way he moved his hips was spectacular. And his gray sweatpants onesie did little to hide the movement of his cock. If anything, the sweatpants accentuated his fantastic member. It was so easy to picture myself on the receiving end of those thrusts.

But rather than running on stage and tearing his monkey suit off, I stayed put and sipped on my banana juice.

Come to mama.

The spotlight followed his every move as he spun around a few times and then jumped off the stage. For a split second I thought he might be headed to the birthday girl's table. But no, of course he wasn't. I was a bride-to-be. And my tits were way better than the birthday girl's. There was no way he'd go to her table first.

He danced up the stairs and put the wooden cloche in front of me.

Thank you, sir.

From afar I hadn't realized how tall he was. It was possible that his height was just an illusion created by the oversized monkey mask, but one look at his banana-colored sneakers told me everything I needed to know. They were *huge.* Size 13 at least. Which made sense, because I'd ordered an extra large. Actually, I'd ordered an extra large *double.* So where was my second man? The only explanation for his absence was that he wanted to make a grand entrance.

The monkey man danced for a second and then pulled the lid off my cloche. To reveal…

A huge banana split. Two bananas. Hot fudge. Nuts. And a dozen scoops of extra extra dark chocolate ice cream. The whole thing was even covered in a white drizzle that must have been the secret sauce.

What the hell is this?!

There wasn't actually supposed to be a banana split under there. The cloche was supposed to be empty. And then the monkey man was supposed to do a whole strip dance and turn his cock into the world's most delicious banana split.

Surely this was a mistake. I turned back to the server as he pulled a can of whipped cream out of his onesie pocket.

There we go!

But instead of putting the whipped cream all over his dick, he squirted a lovely little dollop onto my banana split. And then he danced away.

"That looks fucking amazing!" yelled Ash.

It actually did look pretty good. And based on what I knew about banana parties…there would be plenty more opportunities for me to properly enjoy myself tonight. Not to mention that this banana split would surely go straight to my tits. As far as the girls were concerned, it was basically a giant platter of bread and meat.

I grabbed a spoon and dug in.

Yum.

"Who wants to go next?" asked the DJ.

Ash jumped to her feet. "I DO!!!"

"Crikey she's excited. Someone bring that girl a banana split immediately!"

Another monkey man danced out on stage with a wooden cloche. The spotlight followed him as he danced up to our table.

Ash was already gripping her spoon, ready to dig in.

The monkey man did a little spin and then put the cloche in front of her. But when he opened it, there was no banana split. Just an empty platter surrounded by a bunch of little bowls filled with toppings.

That's what mine should have been like!

He made a big show of picking up the empty platter and staring at it, his giant monkey head tilting to one side in confusion. And then he chucked it into the forest. It hit a tree and shattered into a million little pieces.

"Hey!" said Ash. "Where's my banana split?"

The monkey man danced around a bit more and then unzipped his onesie. His mask stayed on as he peeled the suit off his chiseled body. All the girls cheered at the sight of his rock-hard abs.

And they really cheered when his banana hammock swung free.

This wasn't just any old banana hammock. No…this banana hammock was stuffed to actually look like a banana.

"Ah!" yelled Ash. "Why is he getting naked!?"

He gyrated his hips so that his banana was swinging a few inches from her face.

God, she looked so embarrassed. She was covering her bright red face in both hands. But she wasn't scooting her chair backwards. And she did have her fingers splayed enough to see through them…

The monkey man did a particularly forceful thrust and tore off his banana hammock, leaving him in only his monkey mask and his sneakers.

"Boner," said Slavanka.

Boner indeed. He wasn't as big as Ghost or Teddybear, but he'd make a fine starter for Ash. I loved this for her.

Ash shifted in her chair as he sprayed a thick line of whipped cream along his length. Then he grabbed each bowl of toppings and sprinkled them on his dick, finishing things off with a drizzle of hot fudge.

Ash looked like she needed a bit of encouragement, so I yelled, "Eat it!" And then some other girls took up the chant.

"Eat it! Eat it!"

The monkey man put one foot up on the table to really get his cock close to Ash's face.

She didn't budge.

But the monkey man wasn't ready to give up yet. He reached down, fished a towel out of his onesie, and held it up between Ash and the audience. It created a nice little privacy barrier for her. That way she could eat without anyone seeing.

Is she gonna do it? Normally I would have said no freaking way. But she'd just pounded four banana juices. And I knew that deep down she was a kinky bitch. Most importantly, though, she was a single girl! To not suck it would break like five different single girl rules. Or more, depending on how big he was.

I tried to read the monkey man's body language to determine what was happening behind that towel.

Did his head just tilt back a little? Was that a little thrust of the hips?

If I didn't know better, I'd say that she was doing it!

He dropped the towel. And I could have sworn I saw Ash pulling her mouth off his cock. There were only a few little spots of whipped cream left on it.

I cheered, and all the other girls followed my lead.

Ash immediately put her hand over her mouth. Her eyes were wider than ever.

"Ash!" I yelled. "I can't believe you did it!"

"Did what?" she asked.

"You sucked his cock!"

"I did not! I… He… He wiped it off with his hand to make it look like I did it!"

"Then why is there a little whipped cream on your mouth?"

She snatched the towel from him and wiped her mouth. "There was not!"

"Mhm. Suuuuure."

Our conversation was interrupted by the monkey man dancing between us. He thrust his hips at me and sprayed a line of whipped cream on his cock.

I looked up at him and smiled. "Oooh. Is it my turn?"

He nodded his big monkey mask.

I bit my lip and stared down at his erection. Honestly, it wasn't quite big enough for my taste. Surely if I refused him they'd send someone more to my liking. So I held up my promise ring. "I can't. My fiancé would never forgive me. And I already have a banana split." I shooed him away and took a bit bite of extra extra dark chocolate ice cream.

His shoulders slouched in disappointment as he danced over to another table.

"His banana taste good?" asked Slavanka.

"I didn't blow him!" protested Ash. "And what the hell are strippers doing here anyway? What happened to Single Girl Rule #15: No inviting guys to girls' night?"

Oh Ash. "You're forgetting the second half: ...Unless they're strippers. And anyway, strippers aren't even really boys. They're objects to be used for our entertainment. Just think of them as giant walking dildos. Or bananas!"

"Speaking of bananas...why did you get a real one while I got a stripper surprise?"

"I'm actually not sure why I got a real banana," I said and took another bite of delicious ice cream. "That was unexpected."

"Wait, so all the banana splits are supposed to be cocks?" asked Ash.

"Yeah, girl. Isn't this amazing?"

"Amazing? More like confusing. The narrative at this Banana Party is all over the place. I mean…The DJ is Australian. And she's dressed like she's on some sort of African safari. But then it looks like we're in the jungle."

"Right. And monkeys live in the jungle." It all made perfect sense to me.

"And why are we eating the bananas? Shouldn't the monkeys be eating the bananas? That's like…what monkeys do."

"You want the strippers to suck each other's dicks? Now that would be spectacular entertainment."

"No." She looked horrified by the suggestion. "But that would make more sense. And aren't banana splits an American invention? Oh! And shouldn't the bananas in a banana split technically be cut in half?"

"Dear lord, Ash. Please don't cut their dicks in half."

"Castrate strippers?" asked Slavanka, brandishing a butter knife.

"Let's not," I said. Slavanka was as dangerous to society as she was kinky.

"Okay." She put the knife down.

I turned back to Ash. "So what do you think? Are you gonna touch more of the wildlife even though they warned us not to?"

She took a huge gulp of banana juice and then dramatically pointed to her ear. "Sorry, I couldn't hear you!" she yelled over the music. "What'd you say?"

She had nothing to be embarrassed about. This was a bachelorette party. And even if it wasn't, I would still never judge her for sucking off a stripper. Unless he was ugly. Rule #21: No kissing uggos. That rule clearly included penis kissing.

Either way, it was time to change the topic. I wanted to make sure this girls' night was the best night of her life.

I stared at her and tried to crack the mystery. *What would Ash want to do?* To get inside her psyche, I thought back to my favorite party games when I was 12 years old.

And then it came to me. Honestly, I couldn't believe I hadn't thought of it before.

"Have you ever played truth or dare?" I asked.

This time she heard me just fine. "No! But I've always wanted to. I used to stay up at night thinking of what dares I could make people do. That and spin the bottle always sounded so fun. But I never got invited to any of the cool kid parties. God, what I would have given to play spin the bottle with Archer, Mustang, and Vandal." She looked wistfully into the distance.

Did Ash just admit to wanting to get gang-banged by three dudes with objectively badass names? I knew there was a reason we were getting along so well!

"They sound hot," I said.

"They were. So hot."

"Do you think they became strippers?" I asked. "For all you know, one of them could be hiding behind one of these monkey masks, just waiting for you to come suck their cock." I motioned to the half a dozen strippers wandering around. Most of them were still doing the whole banana split routine, but one of them was just flat-out getting blown.

Ash laughed. "Oh my God, do you really think so?!"

"Maybe."

"Or one is kidnapper," added Slavanka.

I nodded. "That's possible too. Ghostie did say that the Locatelli's enforcer was in town."

"What?!" asked Ash. All the color rushed from her face.

"Why are you so surprised? I told you this right after we got off of the plane. And we talked about it again when we went to fake jail."

"We did?" She looked confused.

Ooooh. She didn't remember. She'd been drunk on banana juice from the flight. Better to play it off. "I'm just joking." *Kind of.* It was entirely possible that the enforcer was here. And if he was, I was ready for him.

"Oh thank God." She looked relieved. And a little more sober than a second ago.

Nope. That won't do. I had to think quickly. And then it hit me. "Have you ever heard of spin the banana?"

"No! What's that?" She leaned forward on her elbows to hear my response. She looked so excited. And just as drunk as before we started talking about kidnappers.

This is gonna be fun. Especially since any minute now they'd surely send me a more well-endowed monkey man to play with.

Chapter 7

SPIN THE BANANA
Friday, Sept 13, 2013

"Spin the banana is a combination of spin the bottle and truth or dare," I said. "Each person gives a dare. And to determine who has to do it, we spin a banana."

Ash's mouth dropped open. "Oh my God. This sounds amazing! Let's play!"

Score! "Okay, we just need a banana." I looked around for one, but there were none to be found. "Damn it. Where are all the actual bananas?"

Ash gave me a sassy look. "See? I told you that my décor was better. And I still think it was a huge missed opportunity for them to not have any banana bread."

"I get banana," said Slavanka. She jumped out of her seat, walked over to one of the fake banana trees, and shimmied right up it. Her ass was everywhere thanks to her super short dress, but she didn't seem to care. She reached the top in record time and yanked one of the banana shaped neon lights off the tree. Sparks flew everywhere as she slid back down. She pulled her dress down and walked back to the table like what she'd done was completely normal.

"Here," she said, plopping the banana down in the center of the table.

"Holy shit, Slavanka!" I reached over to give her a high five. "That was amazing! Where'd you learn to climb like that?"

"Power lines in village break lots. I fix."

"You're a woman of many talents. Maybe we'll learn about a few more during this game." I wiggled my eyebrows at her. It was time to begin. And honestly…there was only one proper way to start a game of spin the banana. "First dare: shove a banana down your throat." I spun the banana.

It spun and spun and spun.

Please land on me.

A rather well-endowed stripper had just walked by. And I very much wanted to shove his banana down my throat.

After like twenty rotations, the banana *finally* started to slow down. It went past Zoraida. Past Esme. Past me.

Damn! Oooh! Is it gonna land on Ash? If it did, it would be the perfect excuse for her to chase down the stripper from earlier. Or to try another.

But alas, it was not to be.

The banana spun *just* past Ash to land on Slavanka.

"I swallow banana?" she asked.

"Yup! Get it, girl!"

She reached across the table, grabbed one of the bananas from my banana split, and shoved the entire thing into her mouth. She legit swallowed it in one gulp.

Ash's mouth dropped. "Slavanka!" she yelled. "That was the coolest fucking thing I've ever seen in my life!"

"Impressive," agreed Esme. "But you better be careful doing that around all these strippers. Last weekend I showed off a similar trick during a flight. Let's just say that the passengers took it as a challenge. My throat hasn't felt the same since."

"You suck Chastity's papa?" asked Slavanka. She mimed a blowjob to really drive the point home.

Of course she has.

"A lady never kisses and tells," replied Esme.

Slavanka shook her head. "No, no. Rule #6: Always kiss and tell."

"Way to quote the Single Girl Rules!" I said. "But it's time for another dare. If you want more info about what happens on Daddy's fun jet, you'll have to ask it in a dare. And then hope the banana lands on Esme or Zoraida."

"No. Ride a stripper." Slavanka spun the banana.

Slavanka, you kinky bitch! I'd been planning to tease the strippers for a while before fucking any of them, but a dare was a dare. And I wasn't one to back down from a dare. The only question was…which stripper would I ride if it landed on me?

It was a hard pass on the one that Ash had blown. Way too small. But at a nearby table there was a stripper wearing dog tags with scars all over his back. And honestly, the girl blowing him wasn't doing a very good job. He'd clearly served our country. He deserved better. And I could certainly give it to him…

But then I looked over at the birthday girl's table, and I knew I'd found my man. I knew I was supposed to be ignoring those lame bitches. But how could I when they had the hottest monkey man? Italian stallion was the only way to describe him. Tall. Tanned skin. Huge muscles. And the moves he was putting on the birthday girl… *Hot damn.* He'd just done some sort of spin move that took the birthday girl from laying on the floor to being bent over in front of him.

The only question mark about him was the size of his cock. He still had his banana hammock on. And while it looked big…it was possible he'd stuffed it.

"It's gonna land on Chastity!" yelled Ash.

I turned back to the banana spinning on the table. It *almost* landed on me. But instead it spun by and stopped on Ash.

Her eyes got huge. "What was the dare again? Something about telling secrets about Daddy's fun jet?"

"Girl, you know what the dare was," I said. "Ride a stripper!"

She took a big gulp of banana juice. And then she gave me a mischievous little grin. "I really get to ride a stripper?"

"Yup."

"I have to admit, I've always wanted to do this…" She stood up and looked right at the hunky soldier.

"Go Ash!" yelled Esme.

Ash strode over to the stripper and politely waited for the girl to finish blowing him. Then she jumped in and whispered something into his over-sized monkey ear.

Is she really going to do it?! Ash being the first girl to suck a cock at the Banana Party was one thing, but being the first to *fuck* a stripper?! That was a big deal. I mean…usually only one or two girls were brave enough to go all the way.

My maid of honor was fucking awesome!

Ash stopped whispering and the stripper got down on all fours.

All fours? Interesting. Was she gonna put something in his butt? Or was I about to learn a new sex position?

Either way, I was here for it.

I leaned forward to watch.

She swung one leg over him and lowered herself onto his back. Almost like she was riding a pony.

Nope, not *almost*. It was *exactly* like she was riding a pony. She smacked his ass and he started crawling towards our table. With Ash on his back.

"Wahoo!" Ash threw both arms in the air and nearly fell off of him. She caught herself by grabbing his left monkey ear. Which made him turn left.

"Wow," I said. "I thought you were gonna ride his dick, but I kind of like this better. Way to treat him like the object he is."

"Yeah! I love riding strippers!" She gave me a high five. Or tried to. Because right before we made contact, we both got distracted by someone yodeling. I looked over as Slavanka rode up to the table on another stripper's back. He was a big hairy bear of a man. Which seemed appropriate, because everyone knows Russians traditionally ride bears instead of horses.

"We race," said Slavanka.

"You're on!" screamed Ash.

"Wait," I said. "I wanna race too!" I looked around for a stripper to ride. There was really only one option: my Italian stallion. He was still giving the birthday girl a lap dance, but whatever. I was the bride-to-be, so I had first dibs on all the strippers. Obvs.

I got to their table just as he tore off his banana hammock. His cock swung out and nearly hit the birthday girl in the face. She pretended to look shocked, but I could tell she was loving it. How could she not? It was a thing of beauty.

And it was mine.

I reached out and grabbed his cock. "Come with me."

"Hey!" said the birthday girl. "Where are you taking him?"

"I'll bring him back in a sec." I had to. Single Girl Rule #38: Every girl deserves a big cock on her birthday. And as much as I hated this bitch, it was her birthday apparently. So I'd bring him back. *If he makes me lose.* If he helped me win, I'd reward him appropriately. Because bachelorettes trumped birthday hos. #You'veBeenTrumped.

The birthday girl whined while I took my Italian stallion by the cock and led him to the dance floor. Ash and Slavanka were already saddled up and ready to race.

"First girl to tag the stage and get back here wins," I said. "And last one back has to do the next dare."

"What's the dare?" asked Ash.

"Well this is your dare, so you get to choose."

"Hmm…" She tapped her finger to her lips. "Oh! I know. Loser has to drink from the banana luge."

"Love it."

"Ready girls?" asked Esme. She and Zoraida had just finished clearing the dance floor to make way for our race.

"One sec." I turned to my stripper. "Here's how this works. If we win, I'll suck your cock until you explode all over my face. If we lose, I'll kick you in the nuts. Got it?"

He nodded his big monkey mask.

"Good boy." I gave his cock one final tug and then pushed him onto all fours.

Esme stood in the center of the dance floor and raised two discarded banana hammocks into the air. "On your marks…"

I sat down on my stripper's back, taking a moment to savor each and every muscle. And since I wasn't a barbarian like Ash and Slavanka, I kept both legs on one side. *Did their equestrian teachers never teach them side-saddle?*

I tugged on my stallion's monkey ear to guide him over to the edge of the dance floor.

"Get set…"

I adjusted my grip on his monkey mask. My first instinct was to go for the ears, but there was actually a little fake tuft of hair sticking up in the middle of the mask. *Well done, Banana Party.* There was a reason I chose to go to a Banana Party for my bachelorette party. It was all about the details.

For a tense moment, we all stared at Esme.

"GO!" screamed Esme, pulling the banana hammocks down to her side with a flourish as if they were checkered flags.

I slapped my stripper's ass and he took off. *Stallion indeed.*

"They're off!" yelled the DJ. She'd turned off the music and decided to do a play-by-play of our race. "Off to a solid start here. Our bride-to-be has taken an early lead. The maid of honor in second. And the bridesmaid is in the rear, already four lengths back. She's really well off the pace here as they make their way into the turn…"

My stallion executed a perfect turn, getting me *just* close enough to touch the stage. As we finished the turn, I got a look at Ash and Slavanka. They were too far back. They didn't have a chance.

I slapped my stallion's ass, but it was more for my enjoyment than to really make him hurry. He was already going as fast as he could thanks to my promise of a blowjob.

"It looks like the bride-to-be is gonna run away with this one," said the DJ. "But wait! What's this? The bridesmaid is making a late move. She's hit the turn hard and she's cut the lead to only 3 lengths. Make that two. And now one! They're neck and neck!"

Slavanka appeared next to me. "Ya!" she yelled as she held onto a big tuft of her stripper's back hair and whipped him in the ass with a thick leather whip.

What the hell? Where did she get that whip?!

"Go boy!" I screamed. I didn't have a whip, but I could still smack my stallion's tight little ass pretty hard.

"With just half the dance floor to go, the bride-to-be is just holding on," said the DJ. "It's gonna be a photo finish…"

I leaned forward to give us a little extra speed. But Slavanka was gaining speed too. I never knew two men could crawl so fast.

Come on, boy! We were so close I could practically taste it. Three feet. Two feet…

And then it all went wrong. My stallion planted his hand right on a banana peel and his arm flew out from under us. Somehow I didn't fall off, but the stumble was enough to slow us down enough for Slavanka to steal the victory.

No!!!

"I'll be stuffed! What a finish!" yelled the DJ. "Just when the bride-to-be was looking like a dinky-di winner, her man slipped on a banana. The bridesmaid wins it. Ace comeback, that."

"I win," said Slavanka as we both dismounted.

"I admit, it was an impressive comeback. But I would have had you if not for that banana peel."

"Yes, yes. Birthday girl sabotage."

I looked over to her table and saw her eating a banana - no peel in sight. She gave me a saucy wave. *That little whore!*

Speaking of little whores…where was Ash? She should have finished by now. I spun around. Poor Ash was sprawled out on the dance floor. She popped right up and ran over to us.

"What happened to you?" I asked.

"My stripper bucked me off. I think I may have kicked him in the ribs too hard. But oh well. That was amazing! Can we go again?"

"You should have smacked his ass," I said. "Or if you had a whip handy, you could have whipped him." I turned to Slavanka. "Where did you even get that whip?"

"I keep in bra."

"Nice. You'll have to show me how you make it fit. But first I need to kick this worthless loser square in the nuts. Spread those legs, big boy."

Instead of spreading his legs, my Italian stallion took off in a dead sprint.

"Hey! Get back here!" I started laughing. I felt bad that he thought I'd really kick him in the nuts. I'd only been joking. I'd never defile such a beautiful specimen of the male anatomy.

"Oh! I'll chase him!" Ash started to run after him, but I grabbed her arm.

"Na, don't worry about it. I promised him a blowjob if we won. And a kick to the nuts if we lost."

"You're SO smart. I can't believe I didn't think to offer my guy a blowjob if we won. Oh well. Losing is fun too. Because now I get to do the next dare! To the banana luge!" She pointed to the bar and then started marching towards it.

Why is she marching? Actually, I didn't care. It looked fun. Slavanka and I marched behind her.

Ash pushed past a few girls and waved the bartender over like a total pro. "One banana slushy," she demanded. "Also, has anyone ever told you how amazing you are at bartending? You make the BEST BANANA JUICE EVER."

"Thanks," said the bartender. "But you have to wait in line for a slushy." She pointed to a line of girls waiting to drink from the banana luge. No, not just any girls. It was the birthday girl and her friends.

They took turns getting on their knees in front of the penis-shaped ice sculpture while the bartender poured banana slushies into the top of it. The slushy slid through the ice and into their mouths.

Gah! First the table stealing, then the banana peel sabotage, and now this? It was impossible to ignore them when they were literally standing in our way. This birthday girl was the worst. But it was fine. By the end of the night, everyone here would know that this was *my* party. Not hers. "Wanna skip this one dare for now?" I asked. "We can always come back to it once the line is gone."

Ash shook her head. "No way! I got this."

"You do?"

Was Ash about to punch a bitch?! That would be amazing. But it wasn't what she did. Instead, she beckoned the bartender back over and said something that I couldn't hear over the music.

The bartender nodded and then handed her a glass of banana slushy.

Ash walked back over to us with the glass in hand.

"It doesn't count if you just drink it," I said. "You have to use the luge. It was part of the dare."

"I know. There are plenty of other luges."

"There are?" I asked. I had only seen the one.

"Mhm. Watch this."

Chapter 8

BANANA LUGE
Friday, Sept 13, 2013

I followed Ash, expecting her to lead me to some hidden bar. But instead she just walked right up to a stripper with pale skin and lean muscles. He had kind of a sexy vampire vibe. If vampires wore monkey masks and had thick, veiny cocks.

"See?" she asked, pointing to his cock. "Another banana luge." She dumped her slushy onto his head and dropped to her knees.

I shared a confused look with Esme.

"Do you think she knows that's a stripper and not a banana luge?" I asked.

Esme shrugged. "No idea. She seems pretty drunk."

Ash opened wide as the stripper stroked his cock. After a minute or so she turned to us. "Why's the slushy taking so long to go through the luge? Is it broken?" She smacked his hip as if that was gonna fix it.

"Try sucking on it," I suggested.

"Oh! Will that help?" She leaned in and did a repeat performance of the Pump Race.

"Damn," said Esme. "That girl loves dick."

I nodded. "She could work on her rhythm a bit, but the passion is certainly there."

It only took about a minute for the vampirey stripper to push her head back.

"Oh!" said Ash. "I think I fixed it!" A thick stream of cum shot into her mouth midsentence. The surprise of it made her jump a little and the stripper's second shot went all over her cheek. But then she adjusted to catch the rest in her mouth.

As was customary at a Banana Party, all the girls nearby cheered her on.

"Yeah!" I yelled as she swallowed the rest of his load. "That's my maid of honor!"

She wiped her face and popped back to her feet. "Yum! I love banana juice, but the slushies are even better!"

"Damn right they are," I agreed. I still wasn't sure if she realized she'd just drank a bunch of cum rather than banana slushy. Either way, she was awesome.

"So what's next?" she asked. "Can we have another stripper race?!"

"That's up to you. You just completed a dare, so you choose the next one."

We headed back to our table and all looked at Ash.

"I'm loving these dares," said Ash, "but I've always wanted to play *truth* or dare. So I dare someone to tell a sexy secret." She spun the banana.

And of course it landed on her.

"Hmmm…let's see. Oh! I know." She leaned forward and beckoned us all in. "So you know when I just drank from the banana luge?" she whispered.

I nodded.

"Well…I don't know if you realized it…but it wasn't really a banana luge. It was actually a stripper. And I just really wanted to suck his cock. He was giving me total Edward Cullen vibes." She hid her face in her napkin immediately after saying it.

"Ash!" I screamed. "You naughty girl!"

She peeked out from behind her napkin. "Do you think anyone knew?"

"No way," I said. "You totally had everyone fooled."

"Oh thank God." She dropped the napkin. "Wait…one more question. Will drinking his cum turn me into a vampire?"

"No," said Slavanka. "Only bite."

"Yeah, that sounds right," agreed Ash.

"So what's the next dare?" I asked.

Ash pointed to herself. "Me again?"

"Yup. As long as you keep doing the dares, you get to keep making them up."

"I love that rule so much. Okay, umm… I dare someone to tell me the dirtiest thing they've done to Chastity's dad on his fun jet." She spun the bottle.

I figured she wanted it to land on Esme or Zoraida. But it landed on me.

"I haven't done anything dirty to Daddy on his jet. It's a shame you didn't ask about the dirtiest thing I've done to one of Daddy's *friends* on his jet, though. That's quite the story… Anyway, my turn!"

I'd had quite enough of these truth dares. We needed some dares that made use of all these naked strippers dancing around.

Hmmm… I took a bite of my banana split while I thought about it. And that gave me the perfect idea. I picked up the tablet and made sure the order was the same as before: Extra-large double with hot fudge, nuts, extra extra dark chocolate, and secret sauce.

"I dare someone to order and eat this banana split." I waved the tablet in the air as I spun the banana.

It started to slow down just after it passed me. I had a feeling it wouldn't make it back to me. And that just wouldn't do.

"Whoa! What's that girl doing?" I pointed to nothing in particular on the dance floor.

While everyone turned around to look, I pointed the banana at myself.

"Oh hey," I said. "Looks like it landed on me. What are the odds?" I grabbed the tablet and hit *order*.

The music faded and the lights dimmed.

"Babes," said the DJ. "Please direct your attention to the stage for two of tonight's featured performers: The Banana Bros." She poked a few buttons on her equipment and a beat started playing that I'd recognize anywhere: Candy Shop by 50 Cent.

"I love this song!" yelled Ash as a spotlight lit up the stage. Then two monkey men danced out. And when I say danced, I mean *danced*.

They weren't just doing the standard stripper dance where they just kind of moved their hips to the beat. No, this was some next level shit.

Every movement was crisp. And they were perfectly in sync with each other. But most impressively…their dancing told a story.

Their moves legit took me to the candy shop.

Well, almost.

The song had been dubbed to be all about a banana shop instead of a candy shop. And the Banana Bros acted it out perfectly.

Their moves were so smooth that they had me soaked before they even took their monkey suits off.

And when they *did* rip their suits off… *Sweet lord.*

Ash gasped as they both did a backflip and somehow lost their suits mid-flip. When they landed, their massive bananas swung forward. It was the perfect move to highlight the biggest banana hammocks I'd seen all night.

The spotlight glistened on their silky-smooth skin as they popped and locked to the music. I just wanted to eat them up. It was like the world's darkest, most delicious chocolate had been poured into molds of the perfect man.

I crossed my legs under the table as they danced up to some girls in the first tier of tables.

It was clear that the girls wanted to lick their bananas, as the song promised they could, but the Banana Bros just teased them.

Good boys.

Their bananas were all mine.

Usually I would have hated waiting while they slowly danced their way up to our table, but in this case, I didn't mind. They were just so beautiful to look at. And each time they thrusted, I got more and more horny. It was a good thing I hadn't worn any panties, because they would have been absolutely *drenched.*

When they finally reached my table, they came straight for me. One of them pulled my chair out and the other started thrusting on top of me. The way his abs tensed with each thrust... *God.*

I reached out and tried to touch his abs, but he somehow stayed just out of my reach.

Such a tease! The more he avoided my touch, the more I wanted to touch him. Or maybe it was just because his abs were freaking amazing. I wanted to lick each muscle.

The other Banana Bro danced on me next. I didn't even bother trying to touch him. Instead I just sat back and enjoyed the show. And by that, I mean I stared at his banana. It looked even bigger close-up. I wanted him to rip his banana hammock off so badly.

He grabbed my thighs with both hands and dropped to his knees. *Oh my God.* I felt the air hit my wetness. I knew he could tell I wasn't wearing any panties. He was looking right between my thighs. Was he salivating behind that mask? I swallowed hard, imagining what his tongue would feel like thrusting inside of me.

But then he was right back up.

Damn it. They were going to make me die of horniness.

The Banana Bros both did a backflip and then tore their banana hammocks off. Their cocks were even better than I imagined.

I'd never seen anything quite like them. They were just as smooth as the rest of their skin. Not a vein in sight. But the real selling point was the length. So. Long. I didn't even understand how they were able to fight gravity and stand upright. But they did.

It took every ounce of self-control for me to not just start sucking them immediately. They'd just teased me. It was payback time. I leaned forward like I was about to put my lips around one of them, but then pulled back. I was running out of willpower fast. I wasn't sure I was even thinking straight anymore.

Luckily I didn't have to wait too long, because the song was almost over.

On the second to last line, someone tossed them each a can of whipped cream. And then they each went into full robot mode and mechanically sprayed a thick line of whipped cream onto the other's cock. The music cut off just as they finished.

The entire club erupted with cheers.

It was by the far the best strip dance I'd ever seen.

And now it was my turn to perform for them.

I opened as wide as I could and took one of them into my mouth, savoring every inch. The whipped cream was delicious. But the cock was better. God, it had been worth every second of waiting.

I only got halfway down before he pressed against the back of my throat. Which wasn't a problem. I shifted a little to fix the angle and took him into my throat. All the way down until my nose was pressed against his tummy.

He groaned and I couldn't help but smile. I was addicted to men making that sound because of me.

When I pulled back, there wasn't a single drop of whipped cream left. I started stroking him as I sucked the other one clean too. Cock and whipped cream were even better than a banana split. It was like my mouth couldn't decide what it wanted to do. So I just went back and forth between the two, like I was sampling ice cream flavors. Spoiler alert – they were both delicious.

"So what's the next dare?" asked Ash, staring at the Banana Bros' cocks.

Oh, that naughty girl. Was she as turned on as I was at the sight of this? There was something about two cocks that really did something to me. And I knew what she was hoping I'd say for my dare, but there was no way I was gonna share these two with her. She could find her own strippers! And as adventurous as she had been tonight, I doubted she was ready for double XL, dark, dark chocolate. These were all mine.

I had to think about my next dare carefully. If I dared one of them to blow a stripper, they might try to steal the Banana Bros from me.

What was a good bachelorette party dare?

Just then, I felt my backup phone vibrate in my bra. It was Chad's special ring tone. Wow, what a mood killer. Actually…I shifted in my seat. Surprisingly it wasn't. I was so turned on that nothing could kill my mood. I didn't even know why it was taking me so long to mount one of these bad boys.

"Uggh, hold on one sec," I said. "Chad's texting." I pulled out my phone and checked the text with one hand as I stroked a Banana Bro with the other. I was so turned on I could barely even see straight. I blinked a few times and made myself focus on the text.

Chad: Can I come hang out with you now? I'm bored.

I'm a little busy. I continued to stroke one of the cocks. "Can someone text Chad back for me?" I asked.

"I dare you to send him a Banana Party selfie," said Ash.

"That's not how spin the banana works. But I like the dare, so I'll do it. On one condition. If I do this, you have to stand up on your chair and give an impromptu bridesmaid speech about how much you love me." I knew that Ash had a deadly fear of public speaking. This was the perfect way to see how drunk she really was.

"Easy. You've got a deal." She polished off another glass of banana juice.

Her sixth? Maybe her seventh.

"You go first though," said Ash. "I need to compose my thoughts."

"Fair enough. What pose do you guys like?" I held up my phone at the perfect angle and made a duck face. But really…the focal point of the image was the two huge cocks on either side of my face.

God they're big. Now I just had to capture their beauty in a selfie.

I snapped a picture. But it was missing something. It felt wrong to not be interacting with the cocks. I grabbed one, licked the other, and took another photo. For a second I got distracted and forgot to even look at my phone. *Focus!* I turned back to my phone.

Much better.

"What do you guys think?" I asked. The girls passed the phone around as I went back to sucking and stroking. I wanted to make sure they were as hard as possible for this photo-op. And the harder they were, the more amazing they'd feel inside of me in a second.

Ash giggled. "I can't believe you'd actually send him this. He's gonna be so mad."

"Why?" I asked. "Single Girl Rule #40: At a bachelorette party, every girl is single again. So it's not like I'm cheating."

"I'm not sure he's gonna see it that way…"

I shrugged. "That's his problem. I told him all about Rule #8. And, well…" I tapped their stomachs as I counted their abs. And then I licked their abs for good measure. *Yummy chocolatey goodness.* I didn't know how, but they even tasted kinda like chocolate.

Speaking of chocolate… "Ohhh!" I said. "I know why you think he'll be mad. It's because he's a racist, right?"

"Chad's a racist?" asked Ash.

"Maybe. He got all weird about me joining an all-black sorority. This'll actually be a good test to see if he's racist or not." I loved chocolate too much for that nonsense. I grabbed my phone back and took another pic of me really going to town on these beautiful cocks. But it still wasn't quite right. "Damn it," I said. "They're so long they don't even look real. And Chad doesn't believe that 8-inch cocks exist in the wild, so if he doesn't see the whole thing, he'll probably just think they're dildos. I know it's not technically a selfie, but can you guys get some pictures from a distance?"

"Yeah," said Ash. "I'm an amazing photographer." She took the phone and started snapping pictures while I sucked off the Banana Bros. I was so glad to have both my hands back. I wanted to touch every inch of these men. And I wanted as much photo evidence as possible of this night so that I could relive it over and over and over again. And also…Single Girl Rule #7: Pics or it didn't happen.

"How do they look?" I asked.

"Pretty good. But I feel like I'm not quite capturing how hot this is." She jumped on the table and snapped a shot at a different angle.

"Oooh! I have the perfect idea." I'd been waiting for this moment all night. I looked up at the Banana Bros. "You guys wanna fuck the bride?" I didn't wait for an answer. It was a yes. Obvs. Their sole purpose in life was to please me. So I just started getting them ready with super sloppy blowjobs. I was soaking wet already, but a little extra lubricant never hurt. Especially with cocks this big.

"Oh shit," one of them muttered. And then cum exploded onto my face from either side.

For a second I was disappointed. I wanted to be railed hard. But...there was no reason to fret. Because the secret sauce was one of the best parts of a banana split. I opened my mouth to catch it, but with them coming from both sides, not much made it into my mouth.

Which was fine. The more cum on my face, the better the photos!

When they were done I smiled and gave two thumbs up for the camera.

First - *yum*. Second - *impressive that they are so in sync that they even cum at the same time.* And third - *Damn it!* Their cum looked amazing on me, but I would have loved for it to be inside of me. Why did I have to be so good at giving head? I'd been so excited to get fucked by them. And now I wasn't gonna get to.

Oh well.

At least I'd gotten good pictures out of it. And there were plenty of other strippers to fuck. I dismissed the Banana Bros, sat back down at my table, and took my phone back from Ash. Yeah, the pictures were perfection. I grabbed a napkin and blotted the cum off my face.

"You're not really going to send one of those pictures to Chad, are you?" asked Ash.

I stared down at the sexiest one. Ash was right. Chad would be so furious that he wasn't the one cumming all over me after he came all the way down to Delaware to visit me. I'd have to show him these photos at just the right time. Like tonight when I got back. Surely they'd set the mood for a really hot night. How could they not? The pictures had me wet all over again.

"Of course I'm going to," I said. But I tilted my phone out of their sight and searched for a picture from earlier tonight. It was between a shot of us on Daddy's fun jet or the one of Slavanka and me smiling on the green with Ash running around in the back. Chad would probably be angry at me for leaving the state when he was visiting. So I decided on the second one. It looked so innocent with the matching pajamas and everything. I added the caption, "Sorry babe, no boys allowed at girls' night." And then I giggled a little. That caption would have been so perfect on the picture of me sucking cock.

But alas…he didn't get to see that yet. I added a winky face and hit send. "Sent."

"Oh my God!" Ash said. "He's going to kill you."

"Ha. Never."

Esme shook her head. "There is no way he's going to be okay with that."

"He'll get over it," I said. His ringtone went off on my phone again. I looked down and smiled. He'd texted back: "Cute."

I looked up from my phone. "He said the photo was cute."

"He have very big cock?" Slavanka asked.

"Eh." If anything, Chad's cock was cute. But I didn't want to say any more so that I wouldn't be caught in a lie. Not that I'd lied anyway. I *had* sent Chad a selfie of me at a Banana Party. Just not this one. And I'd show him the real Banana Party pictures later. #ADareIsADare. I cleared my throat. "Ash, you're up."

"What?" asked Ash as she stared at me.

"You have to give your maid of honor speech." There was no way she could back out now.

"Oh! I almost forgot! Of course!" She hopped up on top of the table and clinked her banana juice glass with a spoon. "Ladies and monkeys! It is with great honor that I introduce the wonderful…the magnificent…the amazing…soon to be Chastity *not* Morgan!"

Wow, this was going to be not good. I put my chin in my hand and smiled. And by not good, I meant epically awesome.

"I've known her for forever," Ash said. "If forever is short. And she's known me just as long. And in that long short time we have become best friends and roommates. She knows me better than my own mother. And she is the most amazingly amazing amazeballs person I know."

This speech made zero sense and I was here for it.

"We are single girls following all the rules. For at least one night. Because alas, she's getting hitched right now. Because pictures were sent. And Chad said cute. And he have very big cock, as the Russians say. And it is my lawful duty under the rule of Delaware legislation to bring this couple to wedded bliss. Do you, Chastity Morgan, agree to bridal things?"

I laughed. "Yes." *What is happening?*

"Then you may kiss the groom!"

She'd acted more like a circus ringleader and a pastor than a bestie, but it was a work in progress. That was why we practiced such things. I grabbed the nearest monkey man's cock and placed a kiss on his tip. *Yummy.*

My table erupted in cheers. But it quickly died away when there was a clinking sound of another glass.

I watched as one of the girls from the birthday party table stood up. "If it's time for speeches, then it's time for the best of the night!"

You dirty whore! Trying to steal my bridal spotlight for a birthday? *Basic bitch.*

"My bestie just turned 21! How fast does time fly!"

Fast apparently, because she looked 50.

"All of us have been friends for forever. And I'm just so emotional tonight as the last of us turns 21."

Friends for forever? I rolled my eyes. That wasn't possible. True friendship didn't even happen until you started following the Single Girl Rules. And there was no way I was sharing them with that group of shrews.

"My bestie is the hottest girl at this party," she added.

"Boo!"

I looked over to see Ash booing at the top of her lungs.

I loved that bitch.

The girl giving the toast made a disgusted noise with her throat. "This table has all the hottest girls in this joint," she said and lifted up her glass. "And we don't even have to try hard to look good. Not like those old chicks getting married up there." She pointed to us.

Oh, hell no.

"Birthday is dumb!" Slavanka yelled, before I could think of something witty to say.

#NailedIt.

"What?" the girl said.

"Birthday is dumb. I no know my birthday. And I am mature person, not child girl."

"You're dumb," the girl yelled back.

Whoa. "Just because my girl speaks broken English does not make her dumb, you ignoramus!" I yelled. "She's learning English and she's fucking kick ass!"

"Slut!"

"Thank you!" I put my hand to my chest. "But you're still a terrible human!"

"Cunt!"

"Language!" yelled Ash. "She said a bad word. Off with her head!"

The microphone screeched as the DJ ran back onto the stage. "Babes, babes. Please. Let's settle this the Banana Party way…with a Banana Race!"

Hell yeah. This was *my* night. *My* Banana Party. I was tired of that birthday girl trying to steal my spotlight. It was time for my squad to show them who was boss.

Chapter 9

BANANA RACE
Friday, Sept 13, 2013

All the girls in the audience cheered the announcement of the Banana Race, but none louder than Ash.

"Wahoo!" She clapped like crazy and then turned to me. "It's a good thing we already practiced riding some strippers. Those dumb birthday girls don't stand a chance."

"This is a different sort of race," I said with a wink.

"Oh." She looked sad for a second, and then recognition flashed on her face. "Right. I think I saw a Banana Race at a Blue Rocks game during the 7th inning stretch one time."

"Did you? Since when do they allow blowjobs at minor league baseball games?"

"No, silly." She tried to boop me on the nose but missed. "Banana Races aren't about blowjobs. Do you think they'll all be wearing banana suits, or will some of them be dressed as other things? God,

I hope none of them are dressed like cucumbers." She shivered.

"What about anything that's happened tonight makes you think that cocks will not be involved in the Banana Race?"

"Oooooh, I love cocks. Tell me more." Ash took a big gulp of her banana juice.

"Bride squad. Birthday squad," said the DJ. "Please join me on stage."

We all got up and made our way to the main stage. The birthday girl and her squad looked like some ragtag team of misfits with their non-matching outfits. Meanwhile my squad was absolutely slaying our pink and white bachelorette theme.

"Before we bring out the bananas, do you wanna know what you're playing for?" asked the DJ.

"Yeah!" yelled Ash.

God, I loved how into this she was.

The DJ pulled a sheet off of a 6-foot-tall golden banana statue. It was magnificent. Exactly the kind of statement piece that our dorm room was missing.

"We of course have the Banana Race trophy. But that's not all. The winning team also wins an all-expense-paid vacation to the one and only Blue Parrot Resort." She held up some tickets and then balanced them against the base of the statue.

Blue Parrot Resort? I'd never heard of it. But it sounded like the perfect place to go for Single Girl Rule #42: Take a girls' trip once a year.

"And now, without further ado…bring out the bananas!"

Ten strippers in full monkey suits danced out on stage and formed two lines, one on either side of the banana trophy.

"The rules of the Banana Race are simple," said the DJ. "Whichever team makes their five men cum first wins. Any questions?"

We all shook our heads.

"Excellent. I'll give you a minute to strategize. Give me a thumbs up when you're ready."

We huddled up.

"Alright girls," I said. "Those stupid birthday bitches have been trying to steal our spotlight all night. But whose Banana Party is this?"

"Ours?" asked Ash.

"What was that?" I asked and cupped my hand to my ear. "I couldn't quite hear you."

"Ours." She said a little louder.

"What?" I yelled.

"OURS!"

"Damn right! This is OUR Banana Party. We're the hottest girls here, and we give the best head. And in a few minutes, everyone is gonna know it. Especially these strippers."

"Which one I suck?" asked Slavanka.

I glanced over at the strippers. They were covered head-to-toe in their monkey suits so we didn't have much information to work with, but the one closest to the trophy was a little taller than the rest and had the biggest feet. "I'll take him," I said. "Why don't we just go down the line from there? Ash next, then Slavanka, then Esme, and Zoraida on the end."

They all nodded.

"Oh, and if you finish first, help out a fellow bridesmaid. Two mouths are better than one." I looked around at my squad. "Thank you all so much for being part of this amazing night. I couldn't have asked for a better group of ladies to suck cocks with."

"Looks like the birthday squad is ready," said the DJ. "Bride squad?"

I held up a finger. I needed one more second.

"This is it. Let's show these bitches how it's done. And remember… Single Girl Rule #23: Never back down from a huge cock. #Fearless on three. One, two, three…"

"FEARLESS!"

We broke our huddle and I gave the DJ a thumbs up.

She nodded. "Alright then. Please take your places in front of your men."

I walked over to my big footed stud and gave him a sexy little dance.

"Hey!" cried the birthday girl. "Is that allowed?"

The DJ ignored her. "Gents, drop your suits."

I eagerly watched my man unzip his monkey suit and let it fall to the floor. There was no banana hammock underneath. Just eight abs and eight thick inches.

He wasn't as long as the Banana Bros, and his skin didn't look nearly as silky smooth. But he had a rugged sexiness. Calloused hands. Thick muscles. A little hair on his chest. I bet the Banana Party scouts had plucked him straight off a farm.

I bit my lip and gave him a little smile to let him know what I thought.

"Whipped cream," said the DJ.

All the men sprayed lines of whipped cream on-to their cocks. Then they tossed the cans aside and put their hands behind their backs.

"Alright, babes. On your mark…"

We all knelt in front of our men.

"Get set…"

I licked my lips.

Instead of saying go, the DJ shot a starter gun in the air and started playing a sick beat.

It was tempting to dive right in and start sucking like crazy, but this wasn't quite like the Pump Race. That was just some inanimate device. Enough pumps with enough pressure, and it would spray you in the face with some water.

But this stripper?

He was a living, breathing sex God of a man. Who got his cock sucked for a living. Which meant a little teasing would go a long way.

I slowly licked the whipped cream off his length, making sure to let a little get on my face. I wanted to give him a nice visual of how his cum would look on me.

Then I flicked my tongue against his tip.

When he thrust his hips forward to get me to start sucking, I knew I had him exactly where I wanted him.

It was time to get started.

I grabbed his ass and shoved his cock entirely down my throat in one swift motion. And then I pulled on his ass to make him go even further. Wow, his butt was so firm. There was something about a tight little ass that did something to me. I was pretty sure I accidentally moaned.

"Oh God," he muttered with a southern twang.

Oh honey, I'm just getting started.

I held him there for a few seconds and then the real fun began. I brought my hands back around, massaging his balls in one hand while the other stroked his shaft in unison with my mouth.

I so badly wanted to reach down and touch myself while my lips were wrapped around his cock. My pussy was just begging for attention. But two hands on him was better than one. I'd just have to be patient. Each thrust in my mouth made me want him inside me even more.

Focus. Hopefully he was thinking about how good this was too. And imagining more just like I was. Like how deep he could be inside of me. How tight I'd be around his thick cock. How wet I was for him. I moaned again. Up and down, up and down. Sucking to the beat. Each thrust of his hips spurring me on even more.

Within thirty seconds I felt him stiffen a little more. And I knew I almost had him.

I took him all the way into my throat again and pushed right behind his balls.

He groaned and thrust forward.

Here we go.

I pulled back, smiled up at him, and gave him a few more tugs.

And I got my reward.

Hot cum exploded out of his beautiful cock, all over my smiling face.

The girls in the crowd cheered, and that just made him cum even harder.

Fuck yeah. Give me that cum. The crowd kept cheering. I was definitely the first to finish. Usually first to finish wasn't the best thing when it came to a man. But in this case…it was perfection.

I wanted to keep sucking him to make sure I got every last drop, but there was no time for such things. My girls needed me.

Desperately, by the look of it.

Actually, half of them were fine.

Esme and Zoraida weren't doing anything groundbreaking, just classic blowjobs with supporting hand action.

But Slavanka and Ash were struggling.

Especially Ash.

What the hell? Seriously. What the hell was she doing? Both her hands were clasped behind her back. Which could have been fine, but instead of really bobbing up and down on him, she was making the weirdest little movement that somehow kept his shaft entirely out of her mouth.

Damn it, Ash! What had happened to her skills from earlier?! Had it just been beginners' luck? Or was this cock just too big for her to handle?

If I wasn't mistaken, Ash had found a third Banana Bro.

Lucky little slut.

"Ash!" I yelled. "What are you doing?! Channel your technique from the Pump Race! You've got this!"

She looked over at me and nodded. And then she started going wild on him. It was good, but she still had no rhythm. And that was the key to getting him over the finish line.

I walked over and ran my hands down her stripper's silky-smooth abs. Then I grabbed his cock and stroked him to the beat.

My hand combined with Ash's mouth was the perfect combo.

"You wanna cum all over my maid of honor?" I whispered into his big monkey ear. "Would you like that, you dirty monkey? Your cum dripping down her chin?"

He nodded his big monkey mask.

"Good boy." I pushed Ash's head off of him with one hand while I stroked him with the other.

She flinched as his cum shot her right in the eye. *Oops.*

I'd aimed plenty of cumshots at my own face, but never at someone else's. I aimed down for the next shot and hit Ash right in the mouth. But this time she didn't flinch. Instead, she opened her mouth and stuck her tongue out. I put the next few shots right on target, filling her mouth with his delicious cum. And then I finished her off with one final shot in her hair.

I'd always wondered why guys liked getting cum in my hair. But now I understood. It was forbidden, and that made it fun.

I wiped some of the cum from Ash's eyes and licked my finger. *No wonder she'd opened her mouth.* All cum tasted good, but this Banana Bro's cum was extra tasty. It was super tempting to put on a nice little show and lick the rest off of her, but the competition was still on.

"And that's a fourth man down for the bride squad," said the DJ as Zoraida pulled back from her stripper with cum pouring out of her mouth. "We're all tied up."

"We need to help Slavanka," said Esme.

No shit.

After seeing her go to down on those sausages I thought she would have been great at this, but... Nope. She was basically just nibbling on the side of his dick. He was getting limper with each nibble.

My first thought was to help him fuck her face, but I was kinda worried Slavanka would bite his dick off. So this called for a different tactic.

"Get behind him and jerk," I told Esme "I'll suck." I ran over and got on my knees. I nudged Slavanka out of the way slightly and gave him a proper suck.

"Hey," said Slavanka. "This my cock."

"I know, but..."

"He no like Russian nibbles?"

Russian nibbles? Was that what she was doing to him? "Uh, no. I don't think so."

"Okay. We suck together." She grabbed my head and pulled me towards her for a kiss. But with his cock in between us.

Slavanka, you kinky bitch! What an excellent use of Single Girl Rule #30: Girl on girl action is only gay if no guys are watching.

He immediately stiffened as our tongues danced around him. There was nothing guys liked more than girl on girl action. Our lips met and we slid down his shaft a few times. I looked up at the monkey mask and winked. *You like that, you bad boy? Two girls worshipping your cock?* It was very possible that if I just started making out with Slavanka he'd cum immediately. But I couldn't get enough of his cock. I needed it deep in my throat. I wanted him screaming my name.

So we each took a turn deep throating him. Meanwhile, Esme played with his balls.

"Make him cum!" yelled Ash.

"Yeah!" agreed Zoraida.

God, I loved my girls. This was officially the best night of my life. Except one thing was missing…

I *still* hadn't gotten fucked yet.

All this cock sucking had me absolutely dripping with desire.

Which made me think…

It was kind of implied that this competition was about giving blowjobs. But was that all we could do? Or were we allowed to fuck them, too?

Because there was no way this stripper would last ten more seconds if I bent over for him.

I was just about to get up and fuck him when he stiffened in that tell-tale way.

Slavanka and I pulled back just in time to get a faceful of his cum.

Esme aimed most of it at Slavanka - it was only fair since this was Slavanka's stripper - but I got a few shots too.

"We have a winner!" yelled the DJ. "The bride squad wins!"

Everyone cheered as we stood up and pumped our fists in the air. I glanced over at our trophy. But what really caught my eye was the gong. Just like cumming in a girls' hair...I knew I wasn't supposed to do it. The DJ had forbidden it.

So naturally, it was all I wanted to do. And the night was coming to an end. Which meant if I was going to do it...

I ran over, grabbed the mallet, and struck the gong. It was way louder than I'd expected.

The lights flickered. And when the palm trees lit back up, they were red instead of green.

A hush fell over the room and the strippers - even the one still getting blown by the birthday girl - all ran away.

"You really shouldn't have done that," said the DJ.

Chapter 10

THE BANANA KING
Friday, Sept 13, 2013

"Gong summon demon?" asked Slavanka.

I wasn't one to be scared of stuff, but… She kind of had a point. There was something quite ominous about this new lighting. And why had the strippers all run off so quickly?

Slavanka pulled me off stage and the rest of my girls followed. The birthday squad had already fled the stage.

We got back into our seats just as *he* arrived.

He was dressed similarly to the other strippers, but there was a golden crown sitting on top of his monkey mask.

And instead of entering through a door, he swung in on some of the vines.

Speaking of swinging…each time he swung, there was something else swinging under that monkey suit of his.

He landed on stage with a thud and beat his chest like a gorilla.

"Who dares disturb me?" he boomed.

I drummed my fingers against my lips and looked away, pretending to be innocent.

The birthday girl was the first one to sell me out. But soon most of the girls in the room were pointing at me.

I pointed at myself and mouthed, "Moi?" As if I had no idea why everyone was pointing at me.

It was all just an act to draw the Banana King over to me, though.

"I told her not to," said the DJ.

"She must be punished," he said in a deep voice.

Oooh, yes please.

"Spank her!" yelled someone.

I was definitely into that.

"Smack her with your cock!" yelled another.

Love it. Keep the ideas coming.

"Throw a banana slushy in her face!"

The fuck? That better have been a euphemism for a cumshot, or someone was being a real dick.

"Fuck her!" yelled someone else. But this time the voice was familiar.

I glanced over at Ash and she gave me a big smile.

Best maid of honor ever.

The Banana King hardly bothered to dance on his way up to our table. He wasn't here to put on a show. He was here on a mission. To punish me.

And I wanted every second of it. I bit my lip as he stopped right in front of me.

He pulled a can of whipped cream out of his pocket and started to unzip his suit.

But before he could get that far, I snatched the can from him.

I'd been licking whipped cream off cocks all night. It was time for someone to return the favor.

I hiked up my skirt, spread my legs, and sprayed a thick glob of whipped cream right on my pussy. Then I gave the Banana King a sassy look.

Your move, big boy.

He didn't hesitate to drop to his knees between my legs. Then he leaned forward and pressed his giant monkey mask into my tits.

No, don't motorboat me, you big dumb monkey! Eat my pussy.

Had the whipped cream not made my desires obvious?

Oh. Oh! I felt his breath on my thighs.

Of course. He wasn't supposed to take his mask off. So the only way he could eat my pussy was to duck under the mask.

And then I felt his tongue lick all the cream off of me.

I swear, I almost came immediately. I'd been so turned on all night I could hardly handle the sensation of his warm mouth on me. I hitched my leg over his shoulder, pulling him closer.

Just like I'd teased the guy in the Banana Race, he used the exact same technique on me. Flicking. Teasing.

I moaned.

He was a freaking pro.

But I didn't want to wait any longer. I'd been slowly dying of horniness all night. It was sinful to be surrounded by so many beautiful cocks and to not have them all inside of me.

So I reached under his mask and ran my fingers through his buzzed hair. And then I pulled him towards me. His tongue slid inside me. And then he swirled it around.

Oh God yes.

The next five minutes were pure bliss.

Chad had eaten my pussy plenty of times, but whatever he'd done was basically the equivalent of Slavanka's Russian nibble technique.

Teddybear, on the other hand, was great at eating pussy. But it always seemed like he was trying to please me.

This was an entirely different experience from both of those.

The Banana King didn't give a shit about my pleasure. He was eating my pussy because he fucking loved the taste of it. I could tell. The way his tongue swirled around me. The way he lapped up my juices. It was like my pussy was the world's ripest, most delicious peach.

He thrust his tongue even deeper, like he couldn't get enough.

Yes!

It went against the Strippocratic oath for him to be so greedy, but I didn't mind one bit. I wanted him to be greedy for me. Desperate for me.

Each stroke of his tongue brought me closer to the edge.

I gripped the back of his head harder and grinded against his face. "Yes," I moaned. *Just like that.*

He pushed his tongue against my clit and my whole body spasmed. But he didn't slow down. Not even a little bit. He just kept feasting.

I moved my arm and I was pretty sure I knocked over a glass of banana juice. But I didn't even care because I was so close to coming again.

And then he stopped.

"Keep going," I demanded. I pushed his head down, but he was too strong for me.

"Sorry," he said as he stood up, his mask falling back into place over his face. "Were you about to come again?"

Fucker! All I could think about was coming again, and he knew it. And then it all made sense. He'd come out to punish me for hitting the gong. And he'd given me the ultimate punishment. One orgasm with no encore.

I knew how to get what I wanted, though.

"You call that a punishment?" I asked, glancing down at his crotch.

Orgasming on his tongue was good. But orgasming on his stiff cock would be better.

I reached up and unzipped his monkey suit. The world's largest banana hammock swung free and hit me in the face.

It was almost comically big. Like, at least a foot. It was more of a plantain than a banana. There must have been so much padding in there.

Or not.

I couldn't believe my eyes as he tore off the banana hammock.

Holy giant cock!

It was the most beautiful thing I'd ever seen.

Longer than the Banana Bros.

Thicker than my farm boy.

And more beautifully tanned than my Italian stallion.

The perfect banana.

No…not a banana. This thing was definitely a plantain. It looked pretty much exactly like one. It even had the same curve. Which would feel *amazing* inside of me.

"Bigger than your groom?" he asked.

I bit my lip and nodded. Then I grabbed his shaft. My hand couldn't even fully close around it. I gave him a few tugs and pulled back.

"No," I said. "I shouldn't. My fiancé would be so mad."

"Says the girl with cum on her face."

"Are you calling me a slut?"

"Yes."

"Hmm…maybe I am. I hope no one tells my fiancé." I grabbed his cock and pulled it towards my mouth. I practically had to unhinge my jaw, but I made it fit. He grabbed my head and pushed me down.

I actually didn't care if anyone told Chad. I was gonna show him those pictures of the Banana Bros. And tell him all about this. Being jealous made Chad so much better at sex.

And it wasn't like I was really doing anything wrong.

There were like five different rules that showed I was clearly in the right here.

First and foremost…Rule #8: If a man has eight abs and eight inches, he may not be refused.

No one was questioning the eight inches. And I was pretty sure he had eight abs.

I opened my eyes to count as I bobbed up and down on his cock. One, two…eight…nine! TEN?!

Did humans even have that many ab muscles? Or was the Banana King some sort of immortal being?

Did immortals have scars? Because he had a few. Including one on his hand. Just like Officer King.

Wait a second!

Officer King. Banana King.

Well hot damn! I knew those cops looked like strippers!

I stopped sucking him off for a second to lick those yummy abs. But when I got up to his massive pecs, I noticed something else.

A shoulder tattoo.

God, could this guy get any hotter?

The tattoo looked so familiar, but I couldn't quite place it. Was it a copy of the Rock's tattoo? More importantly...who cared?

I went back to sucking him. But not too much. My plan was to prove I could deepthroat him and then let him fuck the shit out of me.

I'd already made the Banana Bros and Slavanka's guy cum too fast. I didn't want to repeat my mistake a third time. Especially with the Banana King. To not feel his massive cock inside of me would be a heinous crime.

He pushed against the back of my throat, so I shifted slightly and took him farther. But I still wasn't all the way down.

Gah! How embarrassing.

All the other strippers had run away, so all eyes were on me. This was my time to shine. And I was blowing it. Both literally and figuratively.

I got up and made a show of straddling my chair, facing away from him. Then I leaned back so I was looking at him upside down.

The Banana King was more than happy to put his package on my face.

I sucked his balls for a second while I stroked him.

He flexed and all the girls in the crowd cheered.

Show off.

And then he grabbed his cock and shoved it down my throat. Most girls would have gagged. Or died. Especially the stupid birthday girl. But me? I'd been practicing for this my entire life. I took him all the way into my throat without any problems. Easy peasy. *Thank you, banana deepthroating practice.*

He grabbed my head with his massive hands and fucked my throat. The whole time I was just picturing how amazing it would feel when he did this same thing to my pussy.

It was going to be heaven.

In one swift motion, he reached down, grabbed my waist, and flipped me onto his shoulder tattoo.

Wait a second! I knew where I had seen that design before. It wasn't from the Rock. It was from that picture that Ghost had given me. The one of Locatelli's enforcer.

Oh damn. Silly me, thinking that the Banana King couldn't get any hotter. On the hotness scale, he'd just gone from an 11 to like a…50.

And if he treated me like Ghost promised a kidnapper would… I almost got my second orgasm just thinking about what he might do to me.

"Where are you taking me?" I asked, trying my best to sound worried instead of excited.

"I thought we could have a little fun backstage. Away from prying eyes." He climbed the stairs up to the main stage. In about ten seconds, I'd be backstage and officially kidnapped.

But it wasn't *quite* time for that yet. Because as excited as I was about being kidnapped by this hunk, there was a chance that sex slavery wouldn't be as fun as I imagined.

Like…what if he refused to fuck me?

I know, I know. It was a crazy thought. But I still wanted to be prepared.

Which meant I still needed to get my contingency plan in place. And to get that plan in place, I needed more time.

I glanced back at my table. "Help!" I mouthed.

Ash nodded. And then she yelled, "Fuck her!"

Thank you, bestie. It was like she could read my dirty mind.

"Yeah!" agreed another girl. "Fuck her!"

And then everyone started chanting it.

"Sounds like they wanna watch," I said to him.

The kidnapper put me down on stage next to one of the stripper poles. "Bend over."

"I would. But you know the old bachelorette party rule. A stripper can only fuck the bride if he steals her garter."

"You mean this?" The Banana King reached into his mask and pulled out my garter.

What the hell? I looked down at my thigh. Sure enough, the garter was missing. That cheeky bastard must have snagged it while he was eating my pussy.

And there he went again, getting even hotter.

He slid the garter onto his massive arm. "Now bend over."

Yes sir.

I bent over and grabbed the pole as he bunched my skirt around my waist. Every girl at the Banana Party had crowded around the stage to watch. They were still chanting, "Fuck her." And they were about to get what they wanted. But most importantly…I was going to get what I wanted. The biggest banana at the Banana Party deep inside of me. It was about time. After all, he was the Banana King. And I was about to be the queen of this party.

I arched my back and wiggled my ass for the Banana King.

Someone tossed him a condom. He held it up and looked at it for a moment. Then he laughed. "Save it for her fiancé. They don't make condoms my size."

He grabbed my hips and guided himself into me. Inch by glorious inch.

"YES!" yelled Ash.

But I was even more excited than she was.

I'd never felt so full. And he wasn't even half-way in. My legs were shaking after a few more inches. The slight curve in his cock had him massaging me in a way I'd never felt. Or maybe it was just his insane length. Or girth.

God, he was perfect.

He smacked my ass and I completely lost control. I'd never come so fast in my life. I wasn't even sure he was all the way inside of me yet. It took all my concentration to grip the stripper pole and keep from falling over as I rode out the orgasm.

If he could do that on the first thrust…I was in for a real treat.

He gripped my hips even tighter as he moved in and out of me. "You're so tight," he groaned.

I was pretty sure anyone would feel tight to him. But I always loved that compliment.

His fingers dug into my skin so hard that it hurt. In the best way possible. "Harder," I moaned.

"You little slut." He grabbed my neck and absolutely pounded me against the pole until I came again.

"Did I say you could come?" He tore my dress off, leaving me in only my bride-to-be-sash and my heels.

Naughty boy.

And something about being completely exposed to a crowd and him hissing sinful things at me made me come again, even harder than the first few times.

He grabbed my tits and slammed into me again. And again. And again.

"Is this what you wanted when you hit that gong?" He grabbed a fistful of my hair and tugged. "You wanted me to fuck you in front of a crowd of people like the little slut you are?"

Yes! I was so close to coming again when something caught my eye. Out amongst the trees, I saw big monkey eyes watching me. Wanting me.

So I beckoned him over.

My Italian stallion danced up on stage. Apparently he thought I was no longer a threat since I was bent over getting fucked. And he was right.

As soon as he was within reach, I let go of the pole and grabbed him instead. Then I started sucking him off. And as soon as my lips wrapped around his cock, the Banana King got even harder inside of me. If that was even possible. I kept my lips around the Italian stallion's erection and looked at the Banana King over my shoulder. *You like that? It makes you harder to see me suck a big cock? Are you imagining that it's my lips around you?*

He slammed into me harder.

God yes.

I came again within a few seconds. Two cocks were so much better than one.

And damn, did they know how to use them.

First they took me bent over by the pole, then they got me on all fours. I must have blacked out from the pleasure of it all, because next thing I knew I was flat on my back on a table, surrounded by cocks. I smiled to myself as I realized it was the birthday girl's table. Well…turns out it was my table after all. The Banana King seemed more than happy to share my mouth and hands, but my pussy was all his.

Oh yes. This is gonna be such a fun kidnapping!

It seemed like everything Ghostie had warned me about what true. I wasn't sure why I'd been so worried. Sex slavery was the life for me. I spread my thighs farther apart so the Banana King could fuck me harder. I was never going to get enough of his cock inside of me.

I moaned and my stallion came in my mouth, and another stripper busted in my hand. And then the Banana King got tired of sharing me.

He picked me up and took me back onto the stage, pushing me to my knees.

Time for the grand finale?

He grabbed a fistful of my hair as I eagerly sucked his cock. After all the orgasms he'd given me, I was more than happy to return the favor. But just when I thought he was about to cum on me, he flipped me into a headstand.

The crowd went fucking wild as he drilled me upside down. He'd already gone deeper than I thought possible. But this position took it to a whole new level.

I lost count of how many times he made me come. But it was a lot. God I loved his cock. It was a good thing this wasn't my real bachelorette party, because if it was, I totally would have run away with him rather than marrying tiny-dicked Chad.

Eventually I ended up back on my knees. The Banana King towered above me, stroking his huge cock. Every muscle in his body was so tense.

"Are you gonna ruin my makeup?" I asked.

He nodded.

"What would my fiancé think?"

"I don't give a fuck." And with that, he absolutely *exploded*.

I caught as much as I could in my mouth, but after one shot my mouth was basically full. Cum spilled out onto my tits as he unleashed stream after stream onto my face.

Now this is a cumshot!

My audience seemed to enjoy it just as much, because they were screaming like crazy. Especially Ash. This was definitely *my* Banana Party. I looked over at the birthday girl's table. They were the only girls who hadn't come over to the stage to cheer me on. They were just sitting there looking jealous that I got to have all the fun. One of them was even wiping up some cum that I'd let spill onto their table. *Take that, birthday bitch.*

I swallowed down his cum and then threw my hands in the air to celebrate with them.

"Best night ever!" I screamed. I now understood why the Single Girl Rules were so adamant about having a girls' night every Friday. *I wonder if Daddy will let me borrow his jet so we can come back here next weekend…*

"You're coming with me," said the Banana King. He grabbed my waist and tossed me over his shoulder.

Oh, fun! Kidnapping time!

Chapter 11

MAGIC!
Friday, Sept 13, 2013

"Where are you taking me?" I asked as he carried me backstage.

"To meet a few friends."

Score! This was shaping up to be the sexiest kidnapping ever.

He took a few turns and then we were outside again. But there were no trees or dance floors or bars. Just a helipad.

Oooh, classy. He was planning on whisking me away into the sky!

I looked into the air to see if any helicopters were approaching, but the skies were clear.

"Put these on," said the Banana King.

I spun back to him just as he tossed me a pair of handcuffs. But I didn't catch them. I was too distracted by how hot he looked.

He'd ditched the monkey mask and was back to looking like Officer King. Except he was still fully nude. Well, almost. He'd put his duty belt back on.

He unholstered his pistol and pointed it at my face. "I said put those cuffs on."

And I was soaking wet all over again.

I couldn't help it. Bad boys were my weakness. Especially when they had cocks as big as his.

I bent over in the sexiest way possible and picked up the cuffs. "What are you gonna do to me once I put them on?" The answer, of course, was kidnap me. But it was more fun to play along. And I was hoping he wouldn't be able to resist eating my pussy one more time while we waited for his friends.

"You'll see."

I clicked them on and got them nice and tight. "You have some kinky friends." *I hope.*

As soon as the cuffs were in place, he pulled out his radio. "I've got her. Awaiting extraction. Over."

"Extraction? If I didn't know better, I'd think I was being kidnapped."

"You are."

I gasped. It was probably too dramatic, but whatever. "Are you gonna turn me into your sex slave?"

"No."

What? #Lame. "Then why take me?"

"Because your dad has a lot of money. And my boss wants all of it."

"*All* of it? That's like…a billion dollars." I smiled. I didn't love the idea of him taking Daddy's money. But what he said meant…I was worth a billion dollars. I mean, I already knew that. But hearing confirmation of it was still nice.

"Yup, every last penny."

"I love that plan. But I have a better idea. What if you just keep me as your little fuck toy? Surely my body is worth more than a billion dollars."

"Ha, yeah right. I could buy ten of you for a fraction of that price."

Excuse me? Oh, HELL NO.

I clicked my heels together twice. Like magic, the Banana King's entire body seized up. He dropped the gun as he fell and spasmed on the floor.

Holy shit! That worked way better than I thought it would.

But I didn't have time to marvel at my brilliance. I only had thirty seconds max before the shock would wear off. And then I'd have a very angry, very naked man on my hands.

Which wasn't the worst thing…

He hadn't even been angry earlier and he'd given me the best sex of my life. If anger increased his sexual prowess as much as it did with Chad…

I shivered just thinking about it.

But no…that asshole had dared to insult me. And he was trying to take Daddy's money. And I loved Daddy's money.

So it didn't matter how desperately he'd love another taste of me. As tempting as it was to sit on his face, the moment had passed. Now I was gonna leave him naked on this roof cuffed to a guard rail.

I fished the key out of his belt, unlocked my cuffs, and transferred them to him.

And then he woke up.

He looked around frantically. He stopped and narrowed his eyes at me. "What the hell just happened?"

"Hmm…let's see. You tried to kidnap me. But before you did, I tricked you into taking that garter and putting it on your arm. And that garter happens to be a custom-made shock collar that's linked to a radio transmitter in these bomb-ass shoes. Pretty cool, huh?"

"You fucking bitch."

I gave him my sassiest smile. "Could you please toss me your cell phone?"

"Fuck you."

I clicked my heels together once, sending another jolt through him. "Let's try this again. Toss me your cell phone. Or I'll do two heel clicks. Or maybe three…" I wouldn't actually do three. That would kill him.

With his hand not cuffed to the railing, he grabbed the phone off his belt and tossed it to me.

"Thanks, hun!"

I snapped a picture of him and texted it to Ghost. "Hey Ghostie! Is this the Locatelli's enforcer?"

"Chastity?" he texted back. "Are you okay?"

"Yup, I'm fine," I texted. Then I made a super cute face, gave a thumbs-up, and snapped a selfie. *God I look hot with all this cum on my face.* "But I think he might have ruined my make-up." I sent that along with my cum selfie.

I took a few more selfies while I waited for him to respond. I got a few where you could clearly see my cum-splattered bride-to-be sash. And then I made sure to get one with my kidnapper in the background. His cock had gone completely flaccid from the shock, but it was still huge. He was definitely a shower.

Either that, or he was suffering from the Strippocratic curse. It wouldn't surprise me...I mean, the kidnapping had definitely not been done with my enjoyment in mind. Which meant he'd broken the oath. Which meant his manhood would be forever giant and flaccid. And that would be a great loss for humanity.

I was about to try to seduce him real quick just to make sure his equipment still worked, but two monkey men burst out onto the roof.

Oh! Perfect timing.

"Hey boys," I said. "Wanna fuck me?"

Watching me get railed would be such a fun way to tease the Banana King. And it would also tell me if he was cursed or not. Because that would be the only way that he could watch without getting hard as a rock.

I expected the monkey men to unzip their suits and jump all over that offer, but instead they pulled their masks off.

Ghost and Teddybear.

"I'm so sorry we didn't get here sooner," said Teddybear. "Are you okay?"

"Of course I'm fine. Look at the size of that cock!" I gestured to the Banana King. "I'm pretty sure he made me come like ten times."

Ghost growled.

"What's wrong, Ghostie? Was I a bad girl?" I licked some of the cum off my lips. "You could always put that mask back on and punish me."

Ghost growled again and tossed me a hand towel and a pair of banana pajamas.

I shrugged. "Your loss." I wiped my face off a bit and pulled on the pajamas.

Teddybear looked back and forth between me and the Banana King. "How...?"

"How'd I take him down?"

He nodded.

"Magic!" It was tempting to brag about my brilliant plan with the shoes and the garter, but it was more fun to make him think I had magic powers. "The real question is...what should we do with him?"

"Call the cops?" suggested Teddybear.

"Ew. Don't be such a narc. What if we turn the tables and kidnap *him* instead? Daddy could probably get a nice ransom for him. And until they pay, I'll have a new little play toy."

I said it half as a joke. But the more I thought about it, the more I loved it.

Teddybear did not look excited by the idea. Oh, how I loved how possessive he was. But this wasn't about Teddybear. This was about teaching the Banana King a lesson – to never mess with Daddy ever again.

I was trying to figure out how we could get him back to the plane when a helicopter approached.

No…not just any helicopter. This was a military-grade Blackhawk. A guy in a black ski mask pointed a machine gun at us.

Oh shit.

"Run!" yelled Teddybear. But Ghost had already hoisted me over his shoulder and had me halfway to the door.

The guy opened fire just as we slammed the door behind us.

"Jesus!" I panted. "Was that guy insane? What kind of psychopath would risk damaging my perfect body with bullet holes?"

"A gay one?" offered Teddybear.

"Not a bad thought. But no - even gay men appreciate perfection." I gestured down at my breasts, and then I realized the problem.

I tore off the top of the hideous banana pajamas.

Ghost growled and pulled my top back over my head.

"What are you doing?" I asked. "These damn banana pajamas almost just got me killed! He couldn't see how hot I was or he never would have shot at us."

"This isn't a joke," said Teddybear. "Please just let us get you back to the plane safely. I'd never forgive myself if something happened to you."

"Fine," I sighed. "But I have one condition."

He raised an eyebrow.

"We have to get my friends too. And my banana trophy!" It was officially one of my most prized possessions. There was no way I'd leave it behind.

Chapter 12

ASH'S DADDY FETISH
Early Morning - Saturday, Sept 14, 2013

The pilot's voice on the intercom startled me awake.

"We're beginning our final descent. Please fasten your seatbelts."

Hard pass on the seatbelt thing. I was way too comfy for such silliness. But I appreciated the warning that we'd be landing soon. I needed to thank my friends for the best girls' night ever.

"Girls?" I said. Esme and Zoraida were wide awake doing their flight attendant duties. But Ash and Slavanka were out cold.

I shook them both.

"Huh?" asked Ash, wiping some drool from her face.

Slavanka, on the other hand, shot right up with her whip in her hand, ready to strike.

"Whoa!" I said, putting my hands up.

Her stance softened when she saw it was just me. She gave me a little tsk tsk. "Never startle Russian."

"Right. Ash, you awake?"

She slowly sat up. "Yeah. What's up?"

"I just wanted to thank you girls for the best girls' night ever. No. Scratch that. The best *night* ever."

"Are you kidding?" asked Ash. "Thank *you*. You planned all of that. And while I could have done without the fake arrest, I freaking loved the rest of it. I mean…what kind of party gives you $1200 on your way out the door?"

"I only get $400," said Slavanka with a frown.

Ash rubbed her eyes and looked over my shoulder. "What's going on with them?"

I turned around to look at Ghost and Teddybear. "Oh, just pretend like they're not here."

"I wasn't concerned about them being here. I was more curious about the duct tape, blindfold, and headphones."

"Noise-canceling headphones," I corrected. "I was gonna make them ride in the cargo hold, but Teddybear begged to ride up here. And after they saved my life from that crazy gunman on the helicopter, it seemed mean to not let them. But I also didn't wanna be a bad girlfriend. Can you imagine how pissed Chad would be if he found out that they got to ride with us? I promised him there would be no boys at girls' night."

Ash gave me a funny look. "That seems pretty minor compared to some of the other stuff you did tonight."

"Like what?"

"Uh...all the cheating."

"What cheating? Single Girl Rule #40: At a bachelorette party, every girl is single again. You can't cheat if you're single!"

Ash shook her head. "I really don't think he's gonna agree with that rule. Although I guess he didn't seem too mad about that selfie you sent him. I still can't believe you actually sent him that."

"I actually just sent him a selfie of all of us in our pajamas at your Banana Party. Or...outside of it. When you're were running away from the strippers on the green."

"Hey!" She threw a pillow at me. "I can't believe you lied to us!"

"Technically you just dared me to send a Banana Party selfie. And I did."

"Boo!" yelled Ash. "Lame!"

"Well in my defense, I was planning on showing him the selfies today. I just wanted to show him in person so that he could anger bang me. But after what happened with the Banana Race and the Banana King...I think I'm gonna take a different approach. How fun will it be when he's just surfing Pornhub and sees me on Banana Party's latest video?"

Ash looked super confused. "Pornhub? Latest video?"

"Yeah. I'm not sure how long they'll take to post it, but I'd be shocked if it wasn't up by next month. Don't worry though - I'm on their email list, so I'll be the first to know when they post it. I wonder what they'll call it. I'm thinking *Bride Squad vs Birthday Bitches*."

Ash went ghostly pale.

"What's wrong?" I asked. "You look so pale. Almost like that stripper you pretended was a banana luge!" I reached up to give her a high five. "That was so fucking epic. It'll definitely make the highlight reel."

Ash didn't move.

"Hey, don't leave me hanging."

"Did I just… Did I just star in a porno?"

"Yeah you did!"

"You're joking."

"I'm not."

She looked at Esme. "Is it true?"

"Yeah, girl!"

"Oh my God. OH MY GOD." Her confused look turned into a huge smile. "I'm a porn star! That's so badass." She finally high fived me.

There we go! That was the reaction I'd been waiting for.

"All the guys who ignored me in high school are gonna feel like such idiots when they see it. They missed out. You guys! We're gonna be famous!"

"My parents be very proud," said Slavanka.

Ash's eyes got huge. "Parents... Oh God. Do you think my dad is gonna see it?"

"Oh, for sure. Most of their videos get like 20 million views. He's gonna be so proud of you!"

"No he isn't. He's gonna kill me!"

"Weird. You and your daddy have a strange relationship."

"Are you telling me you'd actually be okay with your dad watching that video?"

"Sure," I said with a shrug. "Why wouldn't I be? It's just sex. Everyone does it. But anyway, they'll use the names from our fake IDs, if they credit us at all. So your daddy probably won't even know it's you."

"But look at me! I'm a ginger. I don't exactly blend in."

"Huh, good point. You do have red hair. And redheaded porn stars are super rare. You're gonna be the talk of Reddit!"

"No! No, no, no! I don't wanna be the talk of Reddit. Are you sure they filmed it? Because I didn't see any cameras."

"They hide them in the trees. And in the monkey masks."

She shook her head. "But...but... Why didn't you tell me?!"

"Because everyone knows about that site. And you signed a release form. You even happily accepted money for your role." I pointed to the envelope with $1200 in it.

"I thought that was a door prize! And the release was to get out of prison!" Ash was breathing so fast. "You can't let them post that video! I'll die!"

"Let me get this straight. You *don't* want them to share that amazing footage with the world?" I didn't understand what was happening. Starring in a Banana Party video was like...the coolest thing ever. "A second ago you thought it was so cool."

"No!" she screamed. "How is my dad seeing me give a blowjob cool?!"

I laughed. She was really hung up on the whole daddy-watching thing. I was beginning to think she had some sort of fetish. "I mean...if he sees you in a Banana Party video and keeps watching, that's kind of on him."

Ash put her hand over her mouth. "Can you open the door? I need some fresh air."

"Uh," said Esme. "We're like 30,000 feet in the air."

"Good! That's high enough to kill me if I jump out, right?"

"Definitely."

"Whoa," I said. I put my hand on her leg to make sure she didn't jump out of the plane. "No need to kill yourself. I promise the footage turned out amazing. Your blowjob on that vampire stripper was so hot. The birthday girls, on the other hand…they probably look like complete idiots. They'll never escape the shame of losing that Banana Race."

"I'm not worried about looking hot!"

Really? "Then what's the issue?" She was being so weird.

"She greedy," said Slavanka. "She want porno all to self."

"Ooooh. Well damn, why didn't you say so? I do kind of like the idea of keeping the footage of our first girls' night as a personal memento. And can you imagine how fun it'll be to show it to guys?"

"Why on earth would I ever want a guy to see it?" asked Ash.

"Imagine if you were dating some guy, and on the third date they told you that they were like…some sort of European royalty. You'd be so excited."

"I guess?"

"And that's exactly how a guy will feel when you show them this tape. They'd be like, *wow, I officially have the hottest girlfriend ever.* And then they'll tell all their friends, and their friends will be super jealous."

"Yeah, no," said Ash. "That's 100% not how it would go. Can you please just make the tape go away forever?"

"Yeah, let me call Daddy. I'm sure he can help."

I pulled out my phone and dialed Daddy.

He answered on the second ring.

"Hi, princess," he said. "Is everything okay? Why are you calling so early in the morning?"

"I need your help."

"Anything."

"Well…me and my new roommate starred in a Banana Party video last night."

"That's amazing! Congrats! I bet you were such a star."

"I totally was. But my friend is feeling a little shy about her performance. So she was hoping you could buy the footage."

"Sure thing. Just forward the details to my assistant and she'll take care of it."

"Thanks, Daddy. Love you. Byyyyye…"

"Princess," he said before I could hang up. "Please tell me that this doesn't mean you took the jet and flew it to Miami when you were under strict instructions not to go out."

"I'm sorry, Daddy. I'll try to remember not to do it again." But I couldn't make any promises. I was very forgetful when it came to ridiculous rules. I loved Daddy, though, so I really would try to be good. If I remembered the rule. Which I probably wouldn't.

"That's all I can ask, princess. I love you."

"Love you too! Bye, Daddy!" I blew a kiss at the phone and hung up. "All fixed," I said to Ash.

"Are you sure?"

"Yup. 100%. Daddy would never let me down. He's not even very angry at me for taking his jet to Miami when I should have been in my dorm. He's very understanding."

She let out a huge sigh. "Oh thank God." She shook her head. "I can't believe you didn't warn us!"

"I swear I thought you all knew. Have you really never seen a Banana Party video? They're so hot." I pulled one up on my phone and started playing one for her. It was pretty good, but ours was gonna be way better.

"Okay, I'd like to propose a new rule," Ash said. "Single Girl Rule #58: No luring your friends onto a porn set."

"Oh Ash. You can't just make up new Single Girl Rules all willy nilly. These are timeless, sacred rules that have been carefully crafted and refined over thousands of years." Also, didn't she know that there were only 44 rules?

"Well can you at least promise me that you won't do it again?"

I smiled at her. "Of course. It can be Best Friend Rule #1."

"Thank you. But also…I'm not sure what that says about our friendship that the very first rule has to be about luring me onto a porn set."

"Uh…it says that we're fucking awesome! In related news…I should probably tell you that next Friday there's like a 50% chance we're gonna end up on a porn set."

"No!" yelled Ash.

"I'm joking. But don't pretend like you didn't have the time of your life tonight."

She turned red and hid behind her pillow. And then she fell asleep.

I patted her head. "Don't worry, girl. Next Friday is gonna be just as epic."

Epilogue

TWENTY?!
Present Day - Saturday - Oct 10, 2026

"Wow," said Ash. "That was quite an outlandish tale. But that's not at all what happened."

"What part did I get wrong exactly?" I asked.

"Uh…the entire second half of the story. I remember that night perfectly. We went to Miami and got caught with fake IDs. And then Teddybear and Ghost came and bailed us out. Craziest. Night. Ever."

"You're forgetting the entire Banana Party."

She looked at me like I was crazy. "Because it never happened."

"Of course it did! I took all 12 inches of the Banana King like an absolute champ. And you got pretty freaky yourself, young lady."

"Yeah…no. None of that is true."

"Yes it is."

"Chastity, I get reminiscing before your wedding. But making up stories? We're going to be late!" She tried to pull me out of the Russian lit aisle of the library.

I pulled my hand out of her grip. "I've told you...shmoopie poo won't mind if I'm a little late for my big day. And I'm not making anything up."

"Prove it."

"Okay." I pulled out my phone and selected a gallery from our college years. "See that 6-foot-tall banana trophy? You know...the one that was in our dorm for 4 years and then in my apartment ever since?"

"Yeah," said Ash. "What about it?"

"Where do you think it came from?"

Ash shrugged. "I always just assumed it was some weird rich person art that I didn't understand."

"What? Why would you think that after the story I just told? Clearly we won it at the Banana Party."

"You're lying. Your story is like some weird fantasy where banana juice is alcohol and it turns me into a wild slut."

I laughed. "Uhh...that's exactly what banana juice is. And let me tell you, it really hits you hard. I've actually documented the stages that you go through while getting drunk on banana juice. After one glass you let loose a little. But you're still terrified of germs."

"Well that makes sense. Germs are terrifying."

"On your second glass, you get even more paranoid than usual. Like when we were getting arrested. You made it such a big thing."

"Right. Because we were getting ARRESTED."

"After three glasses you just love everything. And that's the point of no return. The second you tell me you love me, I know you're gonna get totally shitfaced. Glass four makes you just go nuts, but you still get embarrassed after the fact. Like when you sucked off that vampire stripper. And by the time you're five glasses in, you become the ultimate single girl."

"Which means…?"

"You're down for anything. Especially if it involves big cocks."

"Nope." She shook her head. "I refuse to believe that. You have no proof. I'd never even touched a cock before I met Joe."

I laughed.

"It's not funny! I'm serious!"

"You touched so many cocks before Joe's," I said.

"Lies!"

"You *really* want me to prove it?"

"Yes."

"Okay…" I navigated to the drive on my phone and put in a series of three passwords. Then I scanned my fingerprint. The Banana Party video popped up. "You asked me to never show you this footage again. But you've left me with no other choice." I fast-forwarded to the Banana Race and handed it to Ash.

Her eyes got bigger and bigger with each passing second. "That's…that's not me."

"Keep watching."

She let out a little yelp as the camera zoomed in on me jerking the Banana Bro off all over her face. There was no doubt that it was her.

"No! Make it go away!" She started mashing buttons on my phone until it went back to my home screen.

"Believe me now?" I asked.

She nodded, but she looked completely shook. "So let me get this right. Banana juice is actually alcohol?"

"Yup."

"But I drank it during like every girls' night in college. Good thing I only had like two glasses max."

I laughed. "Girl, you hardly ever stopped at two glasses."

"Yes I did."

"Wait, do you really not remember?"

"No!"

"Holy shit. I knew banana juice made you horny AF, but I didn't realize it actually made you black out. I thought you were just *pretending* not to remember because you were embarrassed about all the cocks you sucked."

"*All* the cocks I sucked?! How many was it?"

"Uh…" I thought back to all the times she'd had banana juice and gone absolutely NUTS. "Maybe 10?"

"Ten?!" she asked. She looked absolutely horrified. I thought she might try to hide behind a bookshelf.

"Aw, don't feel bad. That's a pretty good number. Maybe it was closer to twenty."

"TWENTY!??!" she screamed at the top of her lungs.

A guy poked his head into the aisle with his finger to his lips. "Shhhh."

Ash spun around and held a book out as if it would ward him off. "Stay away from me! I'm a sex pervert."

"It's fine," I mouthed and waved him away. "Ash, you can't go screaming in a library. Especially over this. I'm sure it was at least 15, but then I just remembered that weekend we spent at the Blue Parrot Resort."

"I sucked five dicks in one weekend?!"

The guy poked his head into the aisle again. But this time he looked more intrigued than annoyed.

"Yeah you did!" I put my hand up to high five her. But she left me hanging, so I turned to the guy.

"My bestie sucked five dicks in one weekend! High five!"

He knew that was a good number and high fived me.

"But...but..." Ash started fanning her armpits. "I didn't sleep with any of them, right? I was still a virgin when I got married?"

"That depends. Does fucking a stripper count as losing your virginity?"

"Yes!"

"Then no, you were definitely not a virgin on your wedding night. Actually, you fucked some non-strippers too. There I go again forgetting about that wild weekend in Costa Rica! And that other night. And..." I shook my head. "Are you sure you don't remember any of this? I'm almost certain we've talked about the Banana Party multiple times after the fact."

"We've never talked about this! And I think I'd remember going to the Blue Parrot Resort during college. I know what happens there."

"Yeah you do." I wiggled my eyebrows at her.

She put her face in her hands. "Does everyone else know? Have you told my husband? God, what is he gonna do when he finds out that I'm such a slut?!" With each question she seemed more and more frantic.

"Whoa," I said. "Slow down and breathe."

"Please tell me you're following Single Girl Rule #5 right now."

"Always." I pulled a flask out of the hidden compartment in my dress and handed it to her.

She gulped the entire thing down.

"Feel better?" I asked.

She took a few more breaths and then nodded. "Yeah, a little. I guess everything will be okay. Especially now that I know to never drink banana juice again."

"So uh…about those mimosas this morning."

"What about them? WHAT ABOUT THEM?!"

"They may have had banana juice in them."

Ash stared at me. And stared. And stared.

Did I break Ash?

Eventually she snapped out of it. "How much?"

"Quite a bit. You're probably about two drinks in."

"My paranoid stage?"

I nodded. "That's the one. Which kind of explains your reaction to all this. But it's okay. That third that you just had should kick in soon."

"Third?" she asked, staring at the empty flask in her hand.

"Yeah. Your third banana juice. Just like you asked for."

"I asked for wine! Not banana juice!"

"Well that was very unclear."

"What's gonna happen to me? Am I gonna blow that guy over there? I'm already feeling the urge to do it. I'm going to sex pervert him!"

"Hmm…no. This is definitely still your paranoid stage. I don't think the third drink has kicked in yet."

"I need to know everything."

"Everything?"

"Everything! All the dirty details. What have I done?!"

"Well I would love to sit and chat, but you told me we only had time for one more story. I don't want to be late for my own wedding. And honestly the Banana Party story ended up being like twice as long as I intended. We better hurry back or we're gonna be late!" I pulled the skirt of my dress up like I was about to make a run for the door.

She grabbed my arm. "No. No way, missy! You can't drop that bomb on me and then not tell me anything."

"Are you asking to hear all my stories about the Single Girl Rules? All 44 of them?"

"Yes!"

"I knew you'd come around." I booped her on the nose. "What's next? Ah, yes. Single Girl Rule #3: Never let a friend go into a bathroom alone. That one's especially important for me to remember now that you've had your third banana juice. Who knows what you'd do alone in a bathroom with that handsome stranger?"

"What would I do? Tell me!"

"Okay. Get comfy, because this one is a doozy. If you thought the Banana Party was wild, just wait until you hear what happened in the bathroom during our next girls' night…"

What's Next?

Single Girl Rules Book 3 is coming soon!

But while you wait, you can get your very own Single Girl Rules membership card! And some to share with your friends.

SINGLE GIRL RULES
Official Member

1. **Boys are replaceable. Friends are forever.**
2. Girls' night is every Friday. No exceptions.
3. **Never let a friend go into a bathroom alone.**
4. You can never have too many shoes.
5. **Have wine in your purse at all times.**
6. Always kiss and tell.
7. **Pics or it didn't happen.**
8. If a man has 8 abs and 8 inches, he may not be refused.
9. **If you hear about a well-hung man, share the news.**
10. All celebrations of important life events must involve strippers.

For your printable membership cards, go to:

www.ivysmoak.com/sgr1-pb

The Society

#STALKERPROBLEMS

You know that Chastity is going to get her man (or men…), but what about poor, sweet Ash?

Well I have some good news… Ash has an entire series all about her wild journey to find love! And you better believe Chastity is gonna be there every step of the way to help her.

And yes, Ash is definitely going to still be abiding by the Single Girl Rules. In fact, in the Society, you'll learn about at least 10 more of the rules.

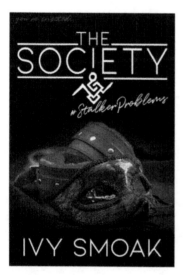

I got an invitation to an illicit club.

They say they'll grant me three wishes.

They say they'll make all my wildest dreams come true.

All I have to do is sign the contract.

Is it too good to be true? I'm about to find out.

Get your copy today!

A Note From Ivy

Bananas really are the best penis-shaped fruit. That was what I was trying to convince you in this wild tale.

But even more important than bananas being #1 - the Single Girl Rules are so much more than a set of rules. They're about finding yourself and having a blast while doing it.

We all thought Ash was this sweet, innocent girl. But get a little banana juice in her system and she really lets loose. Following the Single Girl Rules brings her out of her shell in the best way possible. And that's the power of the Single Girl Rules! So it's time we all embraced them!

And if you think a Banana Party sounds like fun. Oh…just wait until the story behind Rule #3! It's about to get spicy!

Ivy Smoak
Wilmington, DE
www.ivysmoak.com

About the Author

Ivy Smoak is the Wall Street Journal, USA Today, and Amazon #1 bestselling author of *The Hunted Series*. Her books have sold over 2 million copies worldwide.

When she's not writing, you can find Ivy binge watching too many TV shows, taking long walks, playing outside, and generally refusing to act like an adult. She lives with her husband in Delaware.

Facebook: IvySmoakAuthor
Instagram: @IvySmoakAuthor
Goodreads: IvySmoak